Lighted Bridge Publications is a subsidiary of J & G Enterprises

Dedication

This book is dedicated to the memory of an Angel, Ryan Harris, tragically taken July 28, 1998,

"You are a reason for us to continue the fight. You are a shining star, still piercing the night."

And

To my own Black Queen, Malika

"Baby, without you, I would have failed miserably."

CHAPTER 1

I arrived at my office earlier than usual that fateful Thursday morning. It was around 7:30 a.m., June 5, 2002, a day that is permanently etched in my memory. My one story, stucco office building was located on the 2200 Block of Stout Street, on the outskirts of Downtown Denver, Colorado. My charming secretary, Cindy, would not arrive until 9:00 in the morning. My name is Mack and I am a private investigator.

When I entered the building that morning, everything seemed normal. There was no foreboding of the vicious attempt that was going to be made to end my forty-one year old life. Nor had I the slightest premonition that the appearance of the stunningly beautiful, caramel-colored, black queen at my office that afternoon would lead to three deaths, one of which would be dubbed the grisliest murder the city of Denver had ever seen.

I came to work earlier than usual that morning because I could not sleep. Dozing off, only to awaken moments later, I had been lying restless in my bed since 3:43 a.m. I know the exact time because being very time conscious, whenever I awaken in the middle of the night, I always check the time on the luminescent clock that sits on the nightstand. It is always the same melancholy dream that brought my sleep to an abrupt end. My daughter, Melissa, and I were still grieving over the untimely death of her mother and my wife, Jacqueline, whom family and friends had affectionately called Jackie. Melissa, who spent that particular night with her grandmother, manifested her grief by a perpetually sad countenance and a single-minded attachment to her remaining parent; me. In time, our broken hearts would mend. But, at that moment, we were inconsolable. The two things that kept us from being consumed by our misery was our love for each other and the many happy memories we had of our time with Jackie. I was always able to make 10-year-old Melissa smile and laugh by reminding her of some of the funny events from the life that Jackie and I had shared together since we were thirteen years old. We were childhood sweethearts. Melissa looked just like her. No doubt she would grow up to be her twin.

Jackie had been blessed with flawless, mahogany-red colored skin. She was tall for a woman, a statuesque five foot ten. Her eyelashes were naturally long and thick. The irises of her eyes had been the most beautiful shade of golden brown that I had ever seen, and the whites of her eyes were intensely white. I was always amazed and transfixed by their beauty and brightness whenever I looked into them, which was as often as I could. Her hair had been dark red, long and luxuriant. Her lips were full. Her cheek bones were high. Her neck was long and lovely and she had the short, broad nose of a West African beauty queen.

Her character had been even lovelier than her appearance. She had been modest, kind-hearted and giving. Her smile was soft and mischievous. Her laugh was a melody. I really missed my wife. Before her death six months earlier, I had often wondered why God had been so kind to me by bestowing upon me such a beauty. But, after her death, I often found me wondering why God had been so cruel to Melissa and me. Each time, however, I repented.

"The Lord giveth and the Lord taketh away, Mack," had been the words spoken to me by Pastor Harrell in his attempt to allay my grief and explain the tragedy that had devastated my home. In my mind, I knew that the good Reverend was right, but, at the time, my heart could find no solace in his words. The pain had been too deep, the loss too personal.

My grief manifested itself in the recurring dream that awakened me from my sleep time and time again. The dream was a painfully accurate replay of the last moment that Jackie and I had spent together and the last words that we had spoken to each other before she died of an extremely rare and fatal form of stomach cancer. It took her life two shorts months after being diagnosed.

"Mack" she had begun. She never called me anything other than Mack. Not honey not baby, not sweetheart. But she spoke my name with such tender love and affection that I never wanted to hear her call me anything else. I knew instinctively that she was about to die.

"This is it Mack. I can't hold on any longer." She said with sadness in her voice and eyes.

She was heavily sedated with Morphine; otherwise her pain would have been unbearable. Her breathing was shallow and I held her in my arms. For a while, we just looked at each other and cried. Tears streamed down my face and fell on her cheeks and mixed with hers. She didn't want to go and I didn't want her to leave. "I couldn't have asked for a better man. You made me happy Mack!" she whispered. "I love you." Nothing makes a woman happier than when she knows for sure that her man loves and appreciates her. I know you loved me, Mack." As she spoke, we were looking deeply into each other's eyes and into each other's soul. "I love you too and I'll never stop loving you," I said as I struggled to accept that our long life together was coming to a painful end.

Even in her sickness, she was beautiful. The brightness and intensity in her eyes never faded. When she spoke again, her speech was halting and barely audible. I placed my ear close to her lips. "Mack. . . the. . . the . . . Angels . . . Tell Melis . . .tha . . ." Her words ended there and she exhaled for the last time. I cried until the doctor came and the nurses escorted me from the room. And that's how I would wake up after the dream. Tears would be streaming down the sides of my face and I would lie there, like a zombie, before rising from my bed.

How do you say goodbye to a woman whom you have loved deeply and who has shared every meaningful aspect of your life for 28 years? I had torn my mind from thoughts of Jackie and had begun to go over the testimony that I was to give at a trial scheduled for 1 o'clock that afternoon when a foul odor suddenly enveloped the room. At first, I thought the sewer had backed up. The smell was so horrible that I nearly regurgitated my breakfast of turkey bacon, waffles and eggs. The smell became unmistakable. Such stench could only have emanated from one source. It could only have been Almost Dead aka Sinclair Blair, the putrid smelling vagabond, who stalked the alleys and dumpsters of downtown Denver searching for food to eat and cardboard with which to shelter himself at night.

Someone had once described him as looking "almost dead" and like the stench that clung to him, the nickname stuck as well. My eyes confirmed what my sense of smell told me when he appeared in the doorway of my office. I silently cursed myself for having accidently left the back door unlocked. Now the office would have to be aired out, I thought to myself. I did not dislike Almost Dead; it was his repulsive odor, which sickened, me, that I could not stand. Because of his horrible stench, no police officer would arrest him for vagrancy. No one wanted to touch him, let alone put him in their squad car and ride with him to the Adams County Jail. Out of spite, he had once closed down a popular Greek restaurant during lunch hour, the most profitable time of day for that particular establishment. To prevent Almost Dead from rummaging through his dumpsters, the owner of the restaurant had placed locks and chains on them. In retaliation, Almost Dead walked into the man's place of business at the height of lunch hour, took off one of his funky coats and promptly sat down in the middle of the restaurant. The place was empty in a matter of moments. The smell did not abate for hours, thus resulting in the loss of a day's receipts by the owner. He no longer locked his garbage after that.

I had known who Almost Dead was before he had taken on his infamous moniker and had descended into his own personal hell of loathsomeness and funk. Mr. Sinclair Blair, aka Almost Dead, had been the mailman on my block when Jackie and I were living in an apartment on Forest Street in Park Hill, a predominately black, middle-class neighborhood in northeast Denver, where I still resided, albeit in a different home.

Sinclair Blair's descent began when he met a young woman who had gotten him hooked on her body and crack cocaine. She had gotten him hooked, he later told me, so that she could use his steady government check to keep her supplied with crack. I had witnessed him coming later and later each day with the mail. He was more disheveled in his appearance by the day. He was finally fired when he was caught trying to cash a social security check that he had pilfered from the mail. Nevertheless, he did not stop using crack until he had lost everything; wife, kids, house, life's savings, dignity, friends—everything! Even the young woman was dead. She had been stabbed to death in a dispute with another crack addict over a ten dollar rock (piece of crack cocaine).

That had occurred nearly fifteen years ago, yet, Almost Dead had not sought to redeem himself. I believed that he was punishing himself for having allowed his lust and addiction to overcome his intellect and scruples resulting in the destruction of himself, his family and career.

Almost Dead liked Cindy and I because we still addressed him by his proper name and because we fed him doughnuts and coffee from the back door. I assumed that was the reason he was there that morning. I could not have been more wrong! "Ma…Ma..Mack!" Almost Dead greeted me in his stuttering voice as he crossed the threshold into my office. My eyes began to water and I was nearly choked into unconsciousness by the breath that escaped from his rotten mouth. His two or three remaining teeth, which were black, brown and yellow, nauseated me as he looked at me with a ghoulish grin. Almost Dead's eyes were blood shot red and sunken deeply into the sockets. The pitch black circles around his eyes, contrasted by his sickly yellow skin, gave him a face that could only be described as hideous. His hair was filthy and matted on both sides and in the back, but it stood a foot tall in a tangled mess on the top of his head. It had begun to tilt to the right due to its massiveness. He was a sight to behold and, although it was 75 degrees outside, he had on at least, three layers of reeking, filthy rags.

I had not heard him enter the building because his black crusty feet were shoeless. Lord, have mercy; I thought. "What can I do for you this morning Mr. Blair?" I asked Almost Dead as I covered my nose and mouth with one of the monogrammed handkerchiefs Jackie and Melissa had given me for Father's day. "I co..co..come to tell you that a ma..man is lurking 'round your office!" He nearly screamed as he shuffled to the front of my desk. I was nearly overwhelmed with his nauseous odor. I was just about to tell him to get out when I heard the deafening sound of a high caliber pistol being fired at close range. Simultaneously, Almost Dead pitched forward with a gaping hole in his head in the place where his eyes and nose used to be. I was sprayed with fragments of bone and flesh as my instincts drove me to the ground where I quickly dislodged my 44 caliber magnum from my shoulder holster.

The assassin had come in shooting. Poor Mr. Blair was all the way dead now, but I was not ready to leave the physical plane of existence. I had a daughter to raise. I looked under the desk and saw two shoes and ankles walking towards me. Just then, bullets began to splinter the wood from the front of my desk. I needed to take quick and decisive action. The shoes and ankles became my target. I quickly emptied six rounds into them. The owner of the feet cursed and screamed like a captured monkey. He fell to the right as the bullets tore his right foot off. I rolled to the left as I emptied the shells from the magnum and jammed another round into the chamber. I rose up on one knee and began firing in the direction

I knew that target had fallen. In the split second before three bullets slammed into his head and obliterated his face, I recognized the target. It was Clifford Woodson, aka the "Lollipop Rapist" the very man that I was to testify against that afternoon.

CHAPTER 2

I had taken on the case of the "Lollipop Rapist" (as he was dubbed by the media) after six black children from Park Hill were brutally beaten and raped by an elusive, black predator. The police had no solid leads and the community was in an uproar.

Several black community leaders asked me to investigate the case. The Mayor had even given me a call. One black mother interviewed by the local television station expressed what every other black person believed in his or her heart to be true. She said, "If it was lil' white children bein' raped, the police would have been caught the rapist by now!"

I know that the irate woman's comments were not totally unfounded. I had been a police officer in Denver for 10 years before resigning from the force 9 years earlier. I knew that equal value was not placed on black and white flesh. I knew that black men were more likely to be killed by the police than any other race. I knew that the black people committing crimes against whites would receive a harsher penalty than they would if they had committed the identical crime against a black person.

I was an eyewitness to those facts. While things had improved on the surface between the races and more opportunities were open to blacks than ever before, in 2002 there were still people on and off of the Denver Police force who thought that black people deserved whatever ill befell them. There was no distinction between a black victim and a black criminal. In the perverted mind of the racist, all blacks were the same. For blacks, there was still an undercurrent of racism in the "Just Us" system.

I had been just as anxious as any other parent for the "Lollipop Rapist" to be caught. I had not even wanted to imagine how I would feel or what I would do if Melissa were attacked. Ironically, finding out who the "Lollipop Rapist" was proved to be relatively simple; all of the rapes had occurred in Park Hill. This indicated to me that the rapist felt extremely comfortable operating in that area. Based on that indication, I correctly surmised that the rapist was a resident of the community.

Next, the brutality of the rapes suggested to me that the rapist was a repeat offender recently released from prison after serving a long prison term. Several things pointed in that direction. First of all, according to my research, violent pedophilia does not suddenly erupt in the mind of a pedophile. It is a sickness that festers and is nurtured by long periods of unfulfilled cravings and desires. Such would be the case of an incarcerated pedophile. In his sick mind, he wants to hurt and punish the child for not being at his disposal. Secondly, I believed that it was a repeat offender because of what one of the young victims said; "He put a balloon on his thing!" The child was describing a condom. In recent years, persons convicted of sexual crimes and other serious felonies have had to submit their DNA for a state database. The rapist knew that his DNA was on file therefore, he used a condom. No semen was found on any of the victims.

I had my contact at the parole office, Howard Byrd, give me a list of all of the black pedophiles that were paroled into the Park Hill community within six months of the onset of the rapes. There were seven names; six men and one woman.

Next, Cindy and I secretly ascertained the whereabouts of the six men during the time that the children were raped and beaten. All of the rapes had occurred between the morning hours of nine and eleven. Four of them men had rock solid alibis corroborated by several witnesses. The fifth man was eliminated because he was very short and light skinned. He was barely taller than the victims. None of the children had given such a description of the rapist. Virtually all of them had said that the rapist was a big, black man with a beard who wore sunglasses -- an obvious disguise.

That left Clifford Woodson, who had recently been released from prison after serving a seven year sentence for sodomizing an intellectually disabled child. His mother died of a heart attack while Woodson was in prison. He had inherited her somewhat lucrative real estate holdings. This allowed him to live a life of leisure upon his release.

Detectives had interviewed Woodson and others, but they were not able to link him, or anyone else, to the rapes. Woodson was clean-shaven and claimed to have been home sleeping during the mornings of the rapes. He had shown the detectives who interviewed him his extensive classic movie collection, which he claimed kept him up all night and asleep during the day. None of Woodson's statements could be independently verified.

On a strong hunch that Woodson was the "Lollipop Rapist," I began to stakeout his residence on the 3100 block of Hudson. I vicariously disguised myself as a postman, plumber and landscaper. Sure enough, on the second morning of the stakeout, Woodson emerged from his alley wearing a red jogging suit and dark sunglasses. He was beardless. It was difficult to tail him during the day. I often had to let him get two or blocks in front of me. But, I knew he was staking his prey and he would act soon. Judging from the brutality of the previous attacks, his lust had become insatiable. He struck on the fourth day.

I would have blamed myself had he actually been successful because I momentarily lost sight of him that morning as I was tailing him. He had been two blocks in front of me when he turned down 35th and Ivanhoe, one block from Skyland Park. When I got to the top of the block, he was nowhere to be seen. I hurried to the park, where I figured he had gone. It was 9:30 a.m., the park was deserted except for two young girls who were playing on some swings. They both had big lollipops in their hands. In the calmest voice that I could muster, I asked them who had given them the lollipops. "A man," the skinny child with the long pigtails said as she continued to swing and lick her lollipop. "Where did he go?" I asked, as my heart began to pound in my chest. "He took Brenda over there where he keeps his lollipops. Me and Shonda goin,' nex'" she said. "Yeah, he gonna give us some mo'!" the pudgy girl with the red shorts and top nearly sung as she smiled and looked longingly toward the parks' restroom facilities.

I broke into a frantic dash towards the restrooms. I ran straight into the one designated for males. No one was there! I hesitated for half a second before entering the females' restroom and that's where I found six-foot, two hundred and fifty pound Clifford Woodson on top of little Brenda, straining to penetrate her unconscious body. He had donned the phony mustache and beard before entering the park. I couldn't believe my eyes. In my mind, Brenda became Melissa and I went berserk. I kicked Woodson in his face as hard as I could; breaking his nose, fracturing his right cheekbone and dislodging two of his teeth. I then stomped him into unconsciousness. I would have stomped him to death had it not been for the terrified screams of little Brenda Johnson who had regained consciousness and was feeling the physical pain and psychological terror inflicted upon her by Clifford Woodson, the "Lollipop Rapist!"

I handcuffed Woodson and called the police and an ambulance on my cell phone. Little Brenda was petrified and would not move. I covered her with my jacket and called her two friends over to comfort her until the police and ambulance arrived. It was a touching scene as the little girls hugged their friend and told her not to cry. They were mothers in training. That was one year ago. I was to have testified against him that very afternoon. He had a parole hold on him plus a million dollar bond. The parole hold would have prevented him from making bond. I wondered who had gotten him out. There had been no news of an escape from the

Adams County Jail. The answer would not come until later that afternoon.

CHAPTER 3

Four hours after Clifford Woodson killed Almost Dead and then met his own demise at my hands, I was sitting in the lounge area of my office in front of Cindy's desk with Detectives Mike Laraby and Frank Roberts from Area Two Precinct. We were in the lounge because none of us could stand the awful stench that pervaded my private office. The forensics team was still in there with masks on their faces. Almost Dead was now completely dead but his odor lingered on.

Laraby received a phone call from the Superintendent of the Adams County Jail informing him of how Clifford Woodson had managed to be released on bail even though there had been a violation of parole hold on him. His savior was his homosexual lover, Chocolate Delight, whom he met in prison while serving time for a rape involving an intellectually disabled child. Delight had been given power-of-attorney status over Woodson's considerable wealth and had bribed one of the desk officers with $25,000 cash to delete from the jail's computer files the violation of parole hold on Woodson. The female officer had broken down and confessed under pressure. Subsequently, there was a warrant out for Delight's arrest. He was being charged with bribing a public official, aiding and abetting an escape, harboring a fugitive, accessory to murder and attempted murder.

I didn't think they would be able to make the accessory charges stick. They would have to prove that Delight knew in advance that Woodson intended to kill Almost Dead and myself. I made a mental note, however, to keep up with the status of Mr. or Mrs. (as the case may be) Delight who had legally changed his name from Eugene Hadley. "It serves the perverted bastard right, Mack!" Laraby hissed, referring to the violent demise of Clifford Woodson. "It's too bad about Almost Dead though. He sure was an unlucky bastard." "Well, I don't know, Mike," I said. "Maybe he knew it was his last chance for redemption. I just can't stop thinking about the way he grinned at me when he first walked into my office. It was like he knew something was about to happen. You ever grinned at someone when you came to bring them bad news? The way he came and stood right in front of me; it was if he wanted to shield me… My accidentally leaving the back door open... It all seems strange but I know that if it wasn't for Almost Dead, Mr. Blair, I would be lying in that body bag instead of him and my baby girl would be an orphan." A chill ran through me as the reality of my near death settled over me.

I made a written note to myself to have Cindy try to contact members of Blair's family in California. I would pay for the funeral. It was the least I could do for him because he died in my stead. "Mr. Henry, I just want to say that it is a downright pleasure to meet you," Detective Roberts said, addressing me by my surname and extending his right hand. "I have heard many good things about you and I want you to know that I respect you and your work."

Roberts was referring to my efforts and success at finding the evidence that exonerated eight black men and two black women who had been falsely accused and convicted of crimes they did not commit. One of the many reasons why I quit the Denver police and became a private investigator was to help the innocent black men and women who found themselves entangled and about to be mangled by the criminal "just us" system. Court appointed public defenders, who were often referred to as "Penitentiary Deliverers" usually advised their poor clients to cop out (make an agreement for a specified sentence in an exchange for a guilty plea). The problem is that not every poor black person is guilty of the crime charged. The exoneration of hundreds of black men through DNA evidence proves the point. If it were not for the discovery of that science, hundreds of innocent men would still be on death row or languishing in prison cells.

The public defenders who would try to do a good job for their destitute clients were often stymied by case overloads and extremely limited budgets. My paying clients enabled me to take on such cases for free or for a very modest fee in the case of the working poor. Bar none, I am the best in the business. I smiled, shook Robert's outstretched hand and thanked him for the compliment. Detective Roberts was young and country through and through, but he was genuine and had a sharp mind for detail. I could see that by the accurate observations he made while surveying the crime scene and by the meticulous notes he kept. I only hoped that Laraby would teach him how to dress! Roberts had on an ill-fitting green suit that made him look more like a farmer dressed in his Sunday best than a first rate detective in a fairly sophisticated city. His six foot frame and beefy face with blonde hair and blue eyes completed the stereotype. I bet he was often underestimated. Perhaps, that was his intention all along.

In contrast, the black haired Laraby was suitably attired in a dark blue serge suit, white shirt, a red tie and black wing-tipped shoes. It was around one in the afternoon when Laraby and Roberts released the crime scene. Had there been two ordinary citizens shot to death in the office that day, they would have been there half of the night making sure that no detail was missed. As it stood, however, a hated black pedophile and a noisome vagabond were dead. In the case of Woodson, the police were happy and the community was glad. In the case of Almost Dead, no one in the city cared. No one would mourn either of them. Maybe if Woodson's mother had still been alive, she would have grieved over her boy and wondered what she did wrong. From my experience, the good mothers always blamed themselves when the children went wrong. It wasn't their fault; but they always thought there was something they could have done.

Cindy had come in during the time that I was being interviewed by Laraby and Roberts. She had brought doughnuts with her, as usual, but no one had the stomach to eat them because of the horrible stench left by Mr. Blair. It had only begun to abate after five hours of every window in the office being opened. Cindy was sitting behind her desk. I was sitting in one of maroon leather lounge chairs reserved for our clients. I was quietly reflecting on the morning's events. Cindy, in her formfitting white, cotton dress that accentuated all of her womanly curves, began to shake her head from left to right and to sigh repeatedly. When I asked her what was bothering her, she went into a near hysterical tirade. She said, "I swear befo' God, Mack Henry! I swear befo' God you must have some kinda longin' fo' death!" Whenever Cindy was scared or extremely upset, she lapsed into a broken southern dialect. "How many times I done axed (asked) you to keep these damned do's (doors) locked?" She continued to berate me. "Huh? Why you thank (think) I made you install these buzzes and cameras and shit?" I sat amazed and somewhat bemused by Cindy's radical transformation. Her broken dialect and head bobbing and weaving stood in dark contrast to the well-spoken, sedate, demure, self-possessed woman she otherwise was.

Cindy Alice Beasley was one of the most refined women I knew. She was cultured, well-kept, punctual and kind and courteous to a fault. Intellectually, she was my equal, and in some respects, my superior. I didn't mind though. I liked smart women. I often consulted her on cases and deferred to her judgment on many matters. With Jackie no longer on the physical plane of existence, I had come to rely on her counsel and advice in regard to my little princess, Melissa.

In physical appearance, Cindy resembled Gayle King ~ an Amazon queen, Oprah Winfrey's best friend. She was statuesque — about an inch or two shorter than my six foot two inch frame. Her skin was honey brown. Her body was curvaceous and well proportioned. Her hair was light brown and tinted with gold. She was thirty-two years old and quite good looking. Former clients often stopped by just to see her and hear her delightful voice. They would have been astonished to see her then.

I let her vent for a few more minutes before I interjected. I knew she had been shaken by the day's events. I also knew that she was in love with me. She had never spoken of her love for me out of respect for my wife and our marriage, but she manifested it in many other, more subtle ways. Men know when women love them. They may pretend not to, but they know! Nevertheless, Cindy was a lady and never tried to seduce me while my wife was alive. In recent weeks, however, she had begun to make it known in plain and obvious ways that I should not overlook her when I began to search for another mate. Her dresses had gotten a little shorter and a little tighter. Her perfume was sweeter and her demeanor was a little more pleasant than it had ever been. She spoke to me in a voice that often evoked my feelings of passion; the voice that women reserve for their men.

I held up my hand to halt Cindy's tongue lashing and said, "I'm sorry Cindy. I apologize. It won't happen again. It was an inexcusable lapse in protocol. I forgot all about my enemies and our security. I had that dream about my wife again. I've been up since 3:43 this morning and thoughts of her and the impending trail clouded my mind. I already told Cindy about the recurring melancholy dream. Looking into her eyes, I saw her anger begin to subside but the fear lingered. A single tear fell from the rim of her right eye. It twinkled in the sunlight coming from the window and splashed silently onto her desk.

Cindy was beginning to get to me. Her dark brown eyes and her luscious reddish brown, full lips where demanding and receiving my attention. I had not made love for five months. I had recently begun to experience erotic dreams wherein Jackie and Cindy alternately appeared. The nocturnal emissions were a sign from my body that it was in need of some love and affection. I didn't know how much longer I could hold out. I didn't want to introduce another woman into my daughter's life at that time. I knew she was still grieving over the loss of her mother and I feared that she might misinterpret my being in an intimate relationship with another woman as an act of betrayal of her mother. I was in a difficult situation. My physical desires were fighting with my sense of propriety. Cindy blushed as she seemed to read my mind, but she continued to watch me as I assessed her beauty. I was looking at her as I had never looked at her before. I was noticing everything about her; the small vertical scar that graced the corner of her bottom lip, the golden and brown ringlets of her hair that adorned her well-shaped head and concealed and caressed the upper right side of her forehead, the nostrils and bridge of her perfectly formed Ethiopian nose that invited me to caress it with my own, and the faint imprint of her nipples as they pressed against her dress.

I was about to ask Cindy out to lunch, and perhaps something else, when the front door buzzer sounded and nearly startled the desire out of both of us. Cindy frowned and looked annoyed. She had wisely cancelled and rescheduled all of our appointments for the next day. A cleaning crew was on their way to clean my office and to see whether or not the carpet could be saved or would need to be replaced. The awful smell in the office had greatly subsided but a residue still lingered. We were closed for the day, but our walk-in clients didn't know that. "It's a young lady," Cindy said agitatedly after activating the outside camera and switching on her desk monitor.

Cindy had insisted on me having the surveillance equipment installed after an angry husband stormed into the office building one morning to pistol whip me, or worse, for providing his wife with the evidence that he was cheating on her. What he didn't know was that Cindy possessed two pistols of her own which she kept at the ready for just such an occasion. She was also a markswoman who spent five years in the U.S. Army as a M.P. She had attained the rank of lieutenant before retiring to pursue a career in the civilian world. Before the irate husband could kick my door in, Cindy had commanded him, in her authoritative military voice, to drop the weapon. Then she said, "If you don't do it this very second, I'm gonna blow yo' mutha fuckin' brains out!" I put the cuffs on him and Cindy called the police. He seemed to have been relieved when they arrived. There was no doubt in his mind that he came close to dying that day. We had also replaced the glass doors with heavy oak ones and kept the shades drawn as not to provide a would-be assassin with a clear shot.

"Do you want me to let her in or tell her to come back tomorrow" Cindy asked in a voice that seemed to say "send her away and let's finish what you started!" Usually, when people walked into my office without an appointment, they were in desperate need of my help. "Ask her if she can come back tomorrow and see what she says." I said, empathizing with the plea in Cindy's voice and eyes. Cindy activated the outside intercom and said in a very polite voice, "Good afternoon, Miss. Due to an incident that occurred earlier, the office is closed. Can you come again tomorrow?" "I may not be alive tomorrow!" responded a sorrowful response in a childlike voice. It evoked pity from both Cindy and I. As Cindy pressed the button to electronically unlock the front door, I rose from my chair and turned around to see from what person's mouth had come such fear and impending doom. I was astounded by what I saw when the door opened. As the woman walked the twenty paces to where I was standing, I felt that I was in the presence of no less than the Queen Nefertiti herself. She was extraordinarily beautiful and, even in her sadness, her bearing was regal. Draping her five sevenish slender but well-endowed body was a near transparent gold, satin summer dress that barely reached her lovely knees. Her long, jet black, silky hair flowed past her shoulders and was slightly curled at the ends. Her dark caramel skin was without blemish and seemed to glow. The beauty of her hazel brown eyes was arresting. Her nose was medium long, slightly broad and downturned. It was in perfect harmony with her other features. Her full pomegranate colored lips looked delicious. Her long, slender neck was accentuated by a matching satin ribbon she wore as a choker. Her pretty feet were adorned in a pair of gold, strapped pumps that made her legs look even lovelier. She must have incited envy and longing wherever she went. When she stood before me, I could not help but smile and marvel at her beauty. Cindy brought my mesmerizing to an end by clearing her throat. "Please, have a seat, I said." I indicated with my extended arm that she should have a seat on the leather, maroon sofa that sat behind us to my left. She sat down slowly and deliberately like a queen ascending her throne. She then crossed her legs in the most ladylike manner I had ever witnessed. When she was seated, I took a seat in one of the matching chairs opposite the couch. There was a round, wooden coffee table between us covered with half a dozen newspapers and magazines. I looked into the young woman's eyes and said, "Good afternoon miss. I am Mack Henry and this is my assistant Cynthia Beasley. What is your name and, more importantly, who would want to kill you?" "I am Mrs. Valerie Sloane," she said in a very sorrowful tone of voice. "No one wants to kill me, at least not physically. But, if you cannot help me, I will have to kill myself!" After she spoke the last sentence, she signed heavily and began to wring her hands.

CHAPTER 4

What evil happenstance has brought this forlorn beauty to my door and placed her life or death into my hands, I asked myself. Out of all the people and places she could have gone to for help, why had she come to me?

"What help could I render to you, Mrs. Sloane, that would prevent you from killing yourself?" I asked, eager to know what was troubling this young woman to the point that she was willing to kill herself. "You could help me by recovering a pornographic videotape of me that is being used to blackmail me. My husband is Dr. Alfred P. Sloane. If I don't do what the blackmailer says, he's going to release the tape to the media and have it played on the Internet. My husband and his family will be humiliated!" Valerie said as tears began running down her cheeks. Cindy went over to Valerie with a box of tissues and put her arm around her.

Alfred P. Sloane was the most prominent black man in Colorado and the foremost pediatric brain surgeon in the country, bar none. He often traveled out of the state and country to perform, or consult other neural surgeons on the performance of particularly intricate and complex operations, such as the separation of twins conjoined at the head. The black community was justifiably proud of him.

In addition, his great grandfather, Dr. Winston P. Sloane, was a legend in black entrepreneurship. He had come to Denver in the '20s, set up a thriving medical practice and three funeral homes in the black community. It was rumored that he had delivered or buried half of the blacks in Denver during his era, which lasted into the early '60s when ole' Dr. Sloane passed away. My grandfather had told me that they used to say, "If ole' Dr. Sloane don't get you coming, he's sure to get you when you go." In that day, the most prominent blacks of the city, which primarily consisted of doctors, morticians, ministers, lawyers, teachers, and a few business men, lived in the Five Points District on such streets as Ogden and Wellington. But the old Victorian style homes were abandoned by the upper crust in the late '60s when Denver enacted one of the strongest fair housings policies in the nation. While the well to do were able to move into formerly segregated neighborhoods, those left behind had to deal with the economic and leadership void that was left.

In the '70s and '80s the District had become notorious for its poverty and criminal activity. In the '90s and beyond the homes have been reclaimed and refurbished by rich blacks and whites seeking closer proximity to their downtown offices and the expanding amenities of the city.

Winston Sloane had sent all of his sons and daughters to McHerry Medical College in Nashville, Tennessee, which had been established in 1876 to train black physicians. A sex scandal surrounding the family would be a crushing blow to the pride of those blacks who looked to the family as source of inspiration and a validation of the black man and woman inherent intellectual ability and dignity. "Don't cry, honey," Cindy said while she lightly rubbed Valerie's back and shoulders. Cindy didn't have any children but her maternal instincts were strong. She liked Valerie and would, therefore, do everything she could to assist me in helping the young lady out of her troubles.

"Is your husband aware of the existence of this tape and the fact that you are being blackmailed, Mrs. Sloane?" I asked Valerie, as she dappled the tear from her eyes. "No, Mr. Henry, he does not know. That is why I have come to you." Valerie said looking down and placing her hands in her lap. "When I married my husband two years ago," she continued; "He thought that I was a virgin because that's what I told him and because I had my hymen re-sewn seven years ago when I was seventeen. Before I married my husband, I had only had sex with one other man, and that was the bastard who raped me and is now threatening to ruin me and humiliate my husband and his family," Valerie said with bitterness in her voice, I had read about women of Eastern origin who had been sexually active prior to marriage having their hymens re-sewn because of the so-called stigma and shame that attached to the family of a non-virgin. Some women who had sex out of wedlock were murdered by their brothers or fathers in so-called "honor killings." I felt uneasy about a society and a culture that insisted on the chastity of their women but placed no such emphasis on the chastity of their men. Even in this country if a woman has sex out of wedlock she is considered by some to be a slut or whore. No such stigma, however, attaches to her lover or seducer. I'm certain that women resent such double-standards and hypocrisy.

Nevertheless, I was intrigued by the deception Valerie had perpetrated against her husband and wanted to know why she had gone to such lengths to deceive him. But I bided my time. Before asking such a personal question, I waited to see if she would volunteer the information. "You said that you know the person who is threatening to use this tape against you, who is he? How do you know him? And how did he contact you in regards to the tape?" I asked. Valerie Sloane went on to recount one of the most vicious and depraved cases of child abuse and sexual exploitation of a child by a parent that I had ever come across.

From the time that Valerie was 10-years-old, her heroin addicted mother, Annie-Mae Jones, had allowed Valerie to be continuously raped by her drug dealer, Big Pig, for a guaranteed daily dose of heroin. She said that Pig had shown her pornographic movies in preparation for the rape. Her mother had told her that it would only hurt for a little while and that Pig was going to take good care of them from then on. She had also told Valerie that Pig would kill them if she didn't do what he said. I had grimaced at the loss of her innocence and the corruption of her mind.

She had never known her father. She and her mother had lived with Pig and his mother in the Roundville Projects for seven years. During that time Pig had gotten more sadistic and perverse. He would often sodomize young Valerie in her mother's presence. She said that she had only endured the shame and humiliation of her abuse for the sake of her mother, whom Pig had threatened to kill if she ever ran off.

When her mother died of an overdose in 1994, Valerie escaped from Pig's house of horror and found shelter with Mrs. Faheema Shakur, the mother of her best friend, Raheema Shakur.

She said that what she and her mother had endured was relatively mild compared to the bestial acts Pig had subjected some of the other women who were strung out on heroin and crack and could not pay for their drugs with cash or merchandise. I frowned in disgust and my soul ached inside of me when she told me how Pig had made women perform sexual acts with his dog, Duke.

From time to time during my life as a Denver Police Officer, I would hear about drug addicted women being made to engage in bestiality in exchange for drugs. The thought that a black man would subject a black women to such morally debased acts sickened me and enraged me to no end.

I was certain that if I had ever come across any man subjecting any women to such an egregious crime against humanity that I would be facing charges of police brutality or possible murder. It would have entirely depended on my ability to restrain myself at that precise moment.

I felt no kinship with the black man or woman who had no qualms about turning a black woman, one of the most beautiful creatures on earth, into an object of base degeneracy.

I also felt that the black man was failing miserably in his responsibility to protect and respect his woman and to help raise and nurture his children. Whole generations of black children were being raised with no values, morals, or principles. They were easy prey for purveyors of vice.

The government was no better. Instead of trying to intervene into the lives of these children who they knew were destined to become killers, rapist, drug dealers, gang bangers, dope fiends, thieves, armed robbers, burglars, and prostitutes, they vilified the children and built more police stations, prisons and jails to warehouse them in places far away from home where they would not be loved and where their sickness and vices would not be treated but would become more pronounced.

That is another reason why I left the force, all of the efforts and money was being focused on criminal apprehension. No resources were being allocated towards crime prevention. I felt as though the black community was being used to breed criminals for the criminal "injustice system."

Crime does pay, not for the criminal, but for the prosecutors, public defenders, lawyers, judges, stenographers, bailiffs, sheriffs, police officers, prison guards, and other support staff who are living comfortable off of crime and even getting rich and retiring with generous pensions, healthcare and other benefits.

I was now using my skills and intellect to extricate and exonerate the innocent and to unveil and expose the truly guilty. A black man or woman accused of a crime was guilty until they proved that they were innocent. If you couldn't prove that you were innocent, your black ass was going to jail. The same things applied to poor whites, albeit to a far lesser extent.

So far, my investigations had resulted in the release of fifteen innocent black men and women and the incarceration of the real perpetrators of the murders, robberies, and rapes of which they had been wrongfully convicted. But I digress.

It was Faheema Shakur, a devout Muslim, and the receptionist in the office of a corrective surgeon who had convinced Valerie that "In the Lord's eyes, she was still a virgin because she had been compelled against her will," and that she should have her hymen resewn so that her real virginity could be taken by her husband.

Pig had allowed her to go to school where she had excelled in science and math. She received a scholarship to attend a nursing college and graduated four years later a Registered Nurse (R.N.).

She had met Dr. Alfred P. Sloane while attending one of his patients at Children's Hospital. According to Valerie, they had immediately fallen in love and were married six months later. Dr. Sloane, at forty, was her senior by sixteen years.

While her mother-in-law, Mrs. Penelope Johnson Sloane, had initially voiced concerns about her lack of so-called breeding and family background, Valerie had won her over with her personality, beauty, and stated virginity. Penelope Sloane had come to love her and had taught her all the graces and etiquette that she thought she had lacked.

She had become the jewel of the family. Everyone was captivated by her beauty and charm. She had co-hosted several large charity banquets with Mrs. Penelope Sloane at the family's large estate in Lakewood, Colorado, an affluent suburb west of Denver.

She was desperate not to bring shame of the family that had loved her and made her one of their own. She had received a copy of the scandalous videotape in the mail along with a typewritten letter -- both of which she brought to the office. The vulgar letter read:

"You thought you got away from me you stanky ass bitch. I got your funky ass on tape sucking my dick and taking it up your ass. If you don't bring me $100,000, I'm going to put this tape on the Internet and tell your husband what kind of ho [whore] you really is. You know who this is, bitch. You will get another letter from me telling you where to meet me with the money in six days. It won't do your ass any good to go to the po-po [police] because they can't help your ass. Plus, if you do I will still send the tapes to your husband and his friends and put the tape on the Internet for everyone to see what kind of slut Doctor Sloane is married to. If you do what I say I will give you the tapes and you and your punk ass husband can live happily ever after."

I wanted to spare Valerie the embarrassment of watching the tape myself, but I had to know how the tap appeared. I needed to know if Pig's face appeared on the tape and if it appeared that Valerie was being forced or if she was a willing participant. If it appeared that she was being forced, and if things went wrong, Pig could at least be tried for rape, extortion, and blackmail.

To my dismay, however, the tape only showed Valerie performing oral sex on the penis of the man whom she identified as Pig. The sodomy shot was taken from the side and only showed the lower body of the sodomizer but vividly displayed the face and naked torso of the victim who would be heard uttering various sexual obscenities to encourage the sodomizer. It didn't look good. Valerie appeared to be a willing participant.

When questioned about it, Valerie said that she had been forced to say those words. She said that Pig would withhold her mother's daily fix unless she said and did exactly what Pig told her to say and do. Her mother, in the pangs of withdrawal, would beg her to do whatever he asked.

"Please help me, Mr. Henry." Valerie suddenly began to plead, "This tape will devastate my husband and his family. He will hate me for lying to him about being a virgin. He won't believe that I was forced after seeing that tape. I won't be able to face Mrs. Sloane. They will all despise me. My husband will throw me out. I can't live if that happens." As she spoke those last words she began to bawl uncontrollably and to heave spasmodically.

"If he sees that tape, he will think that I enjoyed what happened to me." She continued in the most pitiful voice. "False friends and jealous colleagues will gloat over his humiliation. I won't be able to live with that. I wouldn't be able to bear the fact that it would be I who hurt him so badly. I love that man and his mother with all my heart. Please save me, Mr. Henry. Please don't allow Pig to do this to me! Please!" she screamed and collapsed into Cindy's lap and began to softly murmur like a child who is frightened and hurt.

All of my fatherly instincts and sense of chivalry came to the fore. I was angry as hell that Pig was not content with having robbed the girl of her virginity and childhood. He was now threatening to ruin her entire life. I had no choice but to protect her with all my might. I would be damned before I allowed Pig to humiliate this woman and her family and drive her to suicide.

Cindy was trying to console Valerie by rubbing her back. She said, "Don't cry, sweetheart. It'll be all right. You come to the right place for help. Henry is going to get the tape."

When she said that, she looked at me and communicated with her eyes that I better get the tape. She knew that I would do my best. I went over to the sofa and sat on the other side of Valerie and took her right hand into my hands and said, "Don't worry, Mrs. Sloane. God willing, I will not allow Pig to shame and humiliate you and your family with this vile tape. I will do whatever I have to do to recover the tape. You can count on that. My word means everything to me. What I need you to do now, however, is to get ahold of yourself and your marriage. This is what Pig is counting on. He wants you to get scared and fall to pieces. That puts him in complete control."

Valerie rose up from Cindy's lap and looked into my eye with a faint glimmer of hope. "Do you really think that you can help me, Mr. Henry?" She asked in a voice that was so woeful that it tore my heart in two.

Right then and there I decided that I was going to get that tape even if I had to kill Pig to do it. There was no way I was going to allow that sick child rapist, to further inflict misery on this hopeless young woman. She had escaped from hell. I would feel like a complete failure if I allowed Pig to send her back to it, or kill herself in order to escape the shame and rejection that she would be subjected to if the tape was released to the media.

She had concealed the occurrence of her rape and child abuse. I did not blame her for telling her husband that she was a virgin. In my eyes, she was. "Yes, Mrs. Sloane. I really do think that I can help you," I said.

When I said those words, a beautiful smile brightened her lovely face and she hugged me tight and said, "Thank you, Mr. Henry! Thank you so much?" "But in order for me to help you, I need all of the information on Pig that you could possibly give me," I said.

She hadn't seen Pig in seven years (the day that she fled from him). She said his real name as Dale Chester. That he was fond of dogs. That he used to own several pit bull terriers. That he sold drugs for a living and supported his mother and himself with the proceeds. That his mother's name was Irene Chester and that she had never seen nor heard of his father. The last thing that she said perplexed me. She said that Pig, a.k.a. Dale Chester actually resembled a pig. Little did

I know how truly accurate her description of him would turn out to be.

I told her that once I relieved Pig of the tape that there would be no proof of his allegations. He would be dismissed as insane or worse. That's if he even attempted to say or do anything further after I relieved him of the tape because I fully intended to put the fear of God in him. In addition, there was a warrant out for his arrest. I doubted that he would turn himself in and say that he had been robbed of a pornographic videotape which he had been attempting to blackmail a woman with. Valerie seemed hopeful and relieved before she left my office. I gave her my personal number and told her to call me immediately if there were any new developments in the case.

I escorted Valerie to her late model candy-apple-red Lexus and again assured her that Cindy and I would do our very best to recover the videotape. She hugged me like I was her father and said, "I'll be praying for you, Mr. Henry. I know that God will help you to help me. I don't deserve this. I have been a virtuous woman so long as it was in my power." I watched her drive down South Street until a black Escalade obstructed my view.

CHAPTER 5

After Valerie left, Cindy made a strong pot of coffee. She knew that we would both be up late into the evening plying our contacts for information about Pig. Valerie had received the package the day before. That meant we only had four or five days to find Pig before he contacted her again in regards to the blackmail money. If released into the public, the tape would be viewed as one of the greatest accounts of betrayal and infidelity ever witnessed. I had no doubt in my mind that Valerie would kill herself if that happened. The tape would also do irreparable damage to the pride, hopes, and dreams of the men, women, and children who looked to the Sloane's for inspiration. If I could stop that from happening, I would. But first I had to pick my daughter up from school.

When I pulled in front of Smith Elementary School, Melissa was pouting. I was 3:10 p.m. I was ten minutes late. "Hi baby girl," I greeted her as she tossed her book bag onto the back seat of our late model black Mercedes Benz then grumpily sat down in the front passenger seat. Melissa not only looked like her mother, but she acted like her too. She was giving me the silent treatment for being late. The same treatment that Jackie would give me whenever she thought that I was neglecting her and Melissa by working too much or when I didn't give into her whims about how she should spend our money. In the end it had always worked out. Sometimes I gave in sometimes she gave up.

"I'm sorry that I'm late, sweetheart. Daddy couldn't help it. I had to help a client that's in real bad trouble. There's a bad man that's making her very unhappy." Melissa was tender-hearted like her mother. Hearing of someone else's distress made her relent toward me and break her silence. "You could've called me on my cell phone, Daddy, if you knew that you were going to be late. I was worried about you when I didn't see you when I came out. You could have been somewhere shot or in a car accident or something."

It was apparent that she had studied her mother well. I had hears the same arguments coming from Jackie's mouth. I smiled. She was right and I wasn't about to dispute her logic or trivialize her concerns. "I'm sorry, Honey. I forgot about your cell phone. It won't happen again. Can you forgive your old donkey head Daddy?" Melissa tried to keep from laughing but she couldn't help herself. Her laugh was melodic and infectious. "Yeah, I forgive you, Daddy. Jus' don't let it happen again," she said and grinned mischievously. She knew she was loved.

My little girl was the antidote to depression. I could not help but to be happy when she was happy. Her smile made the day seem brighter and delighted my heart. "Are we going home, Daddy?" Melissa asked as I drove down Thirty-Fourth Street in the opposite direction of our home. "No, baby girl, we're going to pick up Cindy from the office then we're going to Elaine's Pizza Parlor for dinner." "Thanks, Daddy. You know that's my favorite restaurant."

Melissa was smiling in anticipation of eating at Elaine's. She loved Elaine's pizza, and would eat it for breakfast, lunch, and dinner if I allowed her. She would just add fruit and vegetables to the menu. Ever since she was three and her mother told her that she would grow up to be ugly if she didn't eat her fruits and vegetables, you couldn't stop her from eating them. The child would eat half a raw onion and then chase it with an apple and a banana. She had seen Jackie do the same.

Melissa loved her mother and she lived to imitate her. I smiled when I noticed the pink sneakers she had on her feet. They matched well with her light blue cotton pants and pink and white striped Polo shirt. She sported pink and blue ribbons in her dark red hair that was braided into two massive pigtails that hung down her back. She was truly her mother's daughter.

"How's Granny?" I asked Melissa as we drove down Holly Street past Skyland Park. "She's fine. She said she's going to take me to get a training bra Saturday and to let you know." Oh, Lord, have Mercy, I thought. My baby girl needs a training bra. I wasn't ready for that. I was dumbstruck and embarrassed. I glanced at her flat chest and sure enough, two small nubs appeared. It was like it had happened overnight. I wouldn't have noticed if she had not brought it to my attention. Melissa was cheesing broadly, enjoying my embarrassment. All I could manage to say was a lame, "Okay."

Melissa was in a happy mood. She turned the radio on and found KDKO, a black soul music station in Denver. India Arie was singing in a soft sweet voice that seeped into my ears and caressed and soothed my mind. Melissa sung along in her own sweet voice. In spite of everything that happened previously, I thought that it was turning out to be a good day.

When we got to the office, the cleaning crew was already there. The sign on the side of the blue van read: "Mr. Albright's Cleaning Site." "We clean with might, and will work day or night to get things right." Two numbers were listed below the advertisement.

I had already conspired with Cindy to prevent Melissa from knowing about the attempt that was made on my life this morning. I had told Melissa that the office needed cleaning because Almost Dead, a.k.a Mr. Blair had come into my office and died. "Why did he come to see you, Daddy?" she asked. "Did he want some of Cindy's doughnuts and coffee?" "Yeah, Baby Girl." I lied. "He was just sick and tired of being on earth, and it was his time to go," I replied. "Do you think he'll see Mommy in Heaven?" Considering the sacrifice that he made, I thought that it was a good possibility that he would make it to the Pearly Gates. I said, "I'm sure he will, Sweetheart." Then an old scripture I had learned in Sunday school came to mind, "Greater love has no man than that he lay down his life for his brother."

Cindy came out of the building and I was amazed when Melissa climbed into the back seat, allowing Cindy to sit up front next to me. I had known that she liked Cindy, but until that day, I hadn't realized how much. Melissa wouldn't give her mother's seat up to just any old woman. Cindy had to be special indeed.

"Hi 'Lissa," Cindy said as she slid into the front seat. Her long shapely legs momentarily mesmerized me as she pulled down her dress which had rode up to her thighs. I knew she had done it on purpose. Jackie had always managed to keep her dresses and skirts down when getting into the car. Cindy was a mess. She was out to get her man. It was working, too. I was enjoying her company more and more.

"Hi Cindy," Melissa cheerfully responded.

"How's my little girlfriend doing this fine day?" Cindy asked.

"Fine. How are you doing?"

"Oh, I'm doing good, girl. Your crazy Daddy is trying to work me like an old country mule, but I'll be okay."

They both laughed at me. Then I laughed too. Cindy was crazier than I was.

"When's your last day of school, girl?" Cindy asked Melissa as if they had been lifelong friends.

"Tomorrow."

"I know you'll be happy to spend more time with your Daddy at the office."

"Yep, I'm sure looking forward to that," Melissa said gleefully.

I had allowed Melissa to spend some of her summer days at the office with me since she was six-years-old. She loved to answer the phone and play on the computer. But her favorite activity with me was the stakeout, she would insist on wearing all black - like me. And I had to give her, her own binoculars and flashlight. I had never taken her on any dangerous stakeouts just domestic stuff. She has sworn that she was going to be the best detective in the world someday. She loved mystery novels. Her favorite author was Agatha Christy. Melissa was precious. Much more educated and sophisticated than I was at her age. I believed that she would accomplish whatever she put her mind to.

"Mack," Cindy said, diverting her attention from Melissa to me. "The cleaning people said that the carpet can be cleaned and that it will be dry by the morning. They're going to leave several of their large fans on overnight and retrieve them in the morning. They'll be there at nine o'clock."

Cindy knew how to handle her business. That's one of the many things that I liked about her -- she got things done.

"Were you able to allocate any of Mr. Blair's relatives?"

"Only his brother," she responded. He says that Blair's wife and daughter have been informed of his death, but neither one of them intends to come back to attend the funeral. He also thanks you for taking care of the funeral arrangements and to call him when a date is set. He also said that he wouldn't be able to help you with any of the expenses because he's on fixed income."

"When does the morgue intend to release the body?"

"They said that the funeral home can come and get him as soon as possible. I don't even think they did an autopsy of him. They want to get him out of there. I called Sloane's Mortuary. They're picking him up in the morning, but they said there might be some additional bathing expenses. They had already heard of Almost Dead's demise. In fact, no one else but Sloane's would agree to pick him up."

"How much is all this going to cost me?"

"Minus the additional cleaning charges, I selected the $2,000 economy funeral. That comes with a $500 coffin, one hearse, and five minute burial ceremony."

"Thanks, Cindy. As usual, you've done a good job. I don't know what I would do without you," I said.

Cindy beamed and said, "You better recognize!" Melissa laughed and said, "You go girl!" I felt that Cindy and Melissa had established some kind of bond that I was just finding out about.

"Were you able to get any leads on Pig?" I asked, my mind shifting back to that case at hand.

"All that I was able to confirm is that his real name is, in fact, Dale Chester. He has a criminal record a yard long, and has been dealing drugs since he was 13-years-old. He spent the last five years in prison for statutory and was released five months ago on parole, which means that he is still on parole."

Cindy meant statutory rape. Apparently Dale Chester, a.k.a. Pig, had an irrepressible lust for young girls. The chief parole agent, Howard Byrd, was an old friend of mine. I would call him at his office later. He kept a computerized file on the status of all parolees. We had worked together on several occasions when they had lost track of several particularly dangerous parolees. He owed me more than one favor. He had also once hired me professionally in a personal matter.

CHAPTER 6

As soon as Elaine spotted Melissa and me she smiled broadly and rushed over to the table and said, "Mack, you know I don't want you coming into my place without letting me know you here. This baby loves my pizza and I love to see her eating it."

Melissa had begun to laugh almost as soon as Elaine had come to the table. She couldn't help it. Elaine used to make funny faces and tickle Melissa to make her laugh from the time that she was one year old up until about the time she was seven. After Elaine got arthritis she had stopped tickling Melissa when she came into the restaurant, but she always came over to the table to greet us and to let Melissa know that she loved her. Melissa called her "Granny Elaine."

Elaine was the shortest woman I knew. She was not a midget, but I suspected that her roots went back to one of the Pygmy tribes in West Africa. She was browner than a Hershey Bar and her skin looked just as smooth. She wouldn't tell her age, but she had a son who was fifty years old. We had met nine years earlier when she had walked into my office and told me that she was being made to pay $200 a week to a local thug. She had not wanted to have him arrested because she feared that his gang would retaliate against her or her business. She asked me if I would talk to him.

I called my Italian friend, Joe Ziglioni and we paid the young hoodlum a visit. I was in disguise. Ziglioni was sporting a pair of dark shades. We jumped out of the car in front of the gang's hangout; pistol whipped his two so-called bodyguards and threw the gang chief into the trunk of Ziglioni's Cadillac. We took the young thug to a meat processing plant a few miles from the city. Ziglioni took out a bowie knife, unzipped the thugs' pants, and said, "Listen you piece of shit, Elaine is under our protection. If you so much as darken her door step, I'm going to cut your fucking balls off and make hamburger out of them and feed them to my dogs. Do you understand me?" The boy had urinated and defecated on himself. "I swear I won't say nothing to her, Mister. Please let me go. I didn't know she was under your protection." I want the two G's you got from her so far. You better take it to her in the morning and apologize for disrupting her business. You got it?" "Yeah, man. As soon as she opens, I'll take her, her money." The young man did what he was told, quit his gang, and went back to church. Ziglioni was a master of the technique of scaring the feces out of punks.

While Cindy and Melissa ordered our dinner from Elaine, I went to the pay phone to call Byrd. I didn't want to discuss Pig's case in front of Melissa. Byrd's secretary put my call straight through.

"Byrd," he said when he answered the phone.

"Hey, Howie, this is Mack. How's it going?"

"Hey, Mack, what's new? I haven't heard from you in a while. What can I do for you?"

"One of our recent parolees, Dale Chester, is attempting to blackmail a female client of mine with a pornographic tape he made of her under duress seven years ago. She has since that time married a very prominent citizen of this state. The woman is threatening to kill herself if the tape comes out. I don't have any concrete evidence against his as yet. I need his current address in order to setup a surveillance operation."

"I see," Byrd said. "What's his name again?"

"Chester, Dale Chester."

"Just let me type his name into the computer and I should have his information in the database."

I had known that Howard Byrd would not refuse my request for help. Five years earlier I had located and brought home his runaway

14-year-old daughter, Julie, who was on the verge of being seduced into prostitution by a flamboyant pimp, who went by the name of Don Spooky. Spooky only pimped white girls; his tactic was to lavish the runaways with expensive clothes, jewelry, money, and trips to exclusive clubs and restaurants. Once he got them accustomed to that lifestyle, few refused to perform the acts that he said would be necessary to maintain it. He made prostitution fair-seeming and glamorous to the young girls' minds. He didn't tell them that they would be at great risk of being kidnapped, raped, beaten, and that they would be a serial killers favorite prey. Nor did he tell them that they would likely become drug addicts as they sought to numb themselves from the degrading life of prostitution.

To give the girls a hard dose of reality, I would take Sherry Rogers with me when I went to rescue one of them and convinced them that prostitution wasn't glamorous and that they should return to their middle-class neighborhoods where life wasn't nearly so bad. Sherry was one of Don Spooky's former whores. She was only twenty-five years old, but looked as if she was fifty. Half of her teeth had been eaten away by the harsh chemicals found in Crystal Meth, a drug that was beginning to ravage the white community as crack had ravaged the black community. She was H.I.V. positive and weighed only 100 pounds, though she was close to six feet tall. She was skin and bones. I always gave her $300 to scare the hell out of a would-be fool. It usually worked, especially when she showed them a photograph of how beautiful she used to be. It worked on Byrd's daughter. Julie was now in college pursuing a degree in law.

"Bad news, Mack," Byrd said. "Chester is on the run. There is a warrant out for his arrest. He was to be on intensive parole due to the nature of his conviction. Apparently he didn't want the electronic monitoring device to his ankle. He cut it off and fled his mother's home where he was paroled to."

"What is the address that he was paroled to?" I asked.

"4555 York Street, Apartment 3A."

"Isn't that the location of the Roundville Projects?" I asked.

"Yes, I am afraid so. We didn't want him paroled there because of the large number of children residing in those buildings, but no other family member would take him in. His time was up. We had to let him go."

"Thanks, Howie."

"Anytime, Mack. Good luck."

When I got off the phone with Byrd and returned to the table, our pizza, fries, and burgers had already arrived. The food was delicious. I enjoyed being in the company of Melissa, Cindy, and Elaine as we sat cracking jokes and telling Melissa again and again how pretty she was and how much she resembled her mother. Melissa seemed exceptionally happy and Cindy looked exceptionally good. I hated to bring our day to an end, but I only had a few days left to find Pig. If I was going to recover the scandalous videotape, I didn't thing that I had a moment to lose.

It was five o'clock when we left the restaurant. I took Cindy to the office to retrieve her car and to lock up the office. The cleaning crew was waiting for us and presented me with a reasonable bill of $300. I drove Melissa home to get an overnight bag and a change of clothes. She was going to spend the night with Cindy while I went undercover to search for Pig. She and Cindy had worked all that out while I was on the phone with Byrd. I was glad that Melissa had a woman - besides her grandmother - in whom she could confide about her problems and curiosities as a girl-child. I knew Cindy would give her sound advice.

Melissa and I were close, but I knew that there were things that only a woman could teach a girl, and I didn't want her to be deficient in any respect. Cindy lived in a handsome beige and brick ranch house on Monaco Parkway. The former Heavyweight Champion of the World, Sonny Liston, used to live in a house directly across the street. The parkway was picturesquely saturated with maples, spruces, and pines. The dark verdant lawns were well manicured. A red flagstone walk and porch added further attractiveness to Cindy's home. Two twin apple trees stood guard on each side of the lawn. It was a neighborhood of doctors, lawyers, teachers, and other middle to upper class professionals. I felt at ease leaving Melissa with Cindy. I knew that she would protect her with her life.

"Daddy, make sure you call me before my bedtime," Melissa commanded. "You know I can't sleep until I know you're okay." Every day she was sounding more like Jackie. "Okay boss," I said teasingly. "Be expecting my call around nine-thirty or quarter to ten." Melissa hugged me around the neck and kissed me on the cheek before exiting the car. Cindy had come out of the house and was standing outside in front of the passenger side door. She had taken off her white cotton dress and was wearing a white t-shirt with yellow shorts. Her big honey brown legs were smooth and pleasant to behold. She bent over and put her head in the passenger window and said, "Don't stay out all night, Mack. It's been a long day. You need some rest." Her lips were slightly parted and her braless breasts were resting on the door inside the open window. I couldn't tell if she was being deliberately provocative, but I suddenly wished we were married. I'm just going to go by Pig's mother's apartment, have a talk with her, see if she can give me any leads," I said, pulling my mind away from the thoughts provoked by Cindy's sensual pose. "If I come up empty there, I will check with a few contacts in the area. I shouldn't be out too late. I'll call you if anything major develops." "Okay, hon… uh, Mack. You be careful out there. You know you got a daughter to raise," Cindy said while giving me the "you know I love you" look. "I will," I said as I gave her the "we'll be taking real soon" look. I smiled and Cindy smiled and Melissa giggled and said, "Bye Daddy."

CHAPTER 7

On the way to my home on the 3600 block of Fairfax, I contemplated that day's event: I had almost been killed. Almost Dead was completely dead. I made another mental note to make sure that he was properly laid to rest. Clifford Woodson was dead, never to rape again. I was becoming physically attracted to Cindy. I liked her mind and personality. A beautiful young lady desperately needed my help. My daughter seemed to have emerged from her state of perpetual sadness, which had made me even happier. Perhaps a portion of my sadness had been inextricably linked to hers. All in all, it had been a good day; any day that you were almost killed, and not killed, and alive to be counted, was considered a good day.

I turned into the alley between Fairfax and Forest streets and pulled into my two-car garage at 5:46 p.m. I am constantly monitoring the time. If I don't, it seems to slip away from me. I lived in a fairly nice neighborhood. The majority of homes and apartments were built from various shades of brown, red, and beige brick. The lawns were adorned with an abundance of maple, poplar, magnolia, and birch trees. The streets sported such names as Elm, Eudora, Dahlia, Grape, Glencoe, and Ivy.

The neighborhood had previously been entirely white, but when blacks began moving in, in the mid and late 60s, whites began to move out. The few whites who had initially stayed were the older ones whose children had grown up and moved away. Those with children had fled as if they were fleeing the Black Death, a bubonic plaque that swept through Europe and parts of Asia and killed one-fourth of the population in the 14th century.

Racism was more prevalent and pronounced in those days. Things have changed. The city has had both African Americans and Hispanic mayors. Blacks are present in all aspects of city government and are making progress in the economic arena. Nevertheless, pockets of poverty and crime still persist. Naked racism is dead, but its specter still haunts the city.

In 2002, whites were gradually moving back into Park Hill while blacks were slowly moving out. A house that had cost $20,000 in the 60s, was now valued at $250,000 to $300,000. Jackie and I had bought our home almost 15 years prior when the houses were a $100,000 to a $150,000 cheaper.

When I attended Smith Elementary - where Melissa now goes - all of my teachers had been white, except one, Mrs. Lewis. She was African oriented. She wore an afro and beautiful dashiki styled dresses to school. She taught us to love and respect Africa. She taught us well and tolerated no disorder. To this day I have tremendous respect for her. We all knew that she cared about us and had our best interest at heart.

There are four bedrooms in my home - two upstairs and two downstairs. Jackie and I lived in the home for five years before Melissa was born. We hadn't wanted to start a family until we were both settled into our careers; she was an optometrist and I was a police office. When she died, driving home depressed me for a while because she would not be there. Luther was right; "a house is not a home when there's no one there when you turn the key." Jackie had decorated the upstairs and I had decorated the basement. She furnished the living room with very elegant gold and green silk provincial styled furniture. The hardwood floors had been sanded and waxed. Plush green rugs with gold fringes were placed under the couches and love seat. A marble topped coffee table was placed between the two identical couches. On the side of each end chair was a matching marble topped end table with ornate gold lamps with green shades. Whenever we entertained our guests in there, Jackie had received lavish praises for her interior decorating ability.

Melissa's bronzed baby shoes were on the coffee table. Photographs of the family were on every table. Portraits of Malcolm X and Martin Luther King, Jr. were placed beside each other on the north wall. On the south wall was a stunning portrait of Jackie. The dining room contained a large mahogany dinner table that seated eight. It was also made in the French provincial style with gold embroidered cushions on the chair. Above the dining room table was a small crystal chandelier that made the china cabinet sparkle like polished gems.

Our kitchen had been remodeled by professionals. Carved pine cabinets covered the upper portions of the east and west walls. An oven and range stood under the cabinets on the east and matching bronze colored refrigerator and freezer stood along the west wall. The double sink was equipped with a garbage disposal. There was a dishwasher just to the left of the sink. The counters were granite topped and so was our small kitchen table. That is where Jackie, Melissa and I used to eat most of our meals. Melissa and I carry on the tradition. The dining room is reserved for very special occasions.

I descended the uncarpeted wooden stairs to the basement which, in addition to the two bedrooms, contained a bathroom with shower, laundry room, and my study in the den. I had paneled every room except the laundry room with red oak. My shelves were full of dictionaries, encyclopedias, history books, political science books, criminology and psychology books, and hundreds of novels and how-to books. Melissa's extensive collection of Agatha Christy novels had made it to my shelves. She loved to come into my study to pester me and pretend that she was working on cases of her own.

Jackie had claimed that she didn't like the basement. She only pretended not to like it because she had not decorated it. That was one of the few instances in which she didn't get her way. I didn't want her feminine touch in my den. She would have had me on delicate sofas and chairs. I need a place where I could stretch out and be comfortable. In retaliation, she only came down the stairs to do the laundry and to spy on me. When I say spy on me, I mean that in a playful way. She just always wanted to know what I was reading, what I was working on, and how my cases were coming along. She never lost interest in me and I never lost interest in her.

At my desk was a big leather recliner. There were two matching brown leather sofas along the east and sough walls. A hundred photographs of various family members covered the west wall. The large bedroom was reserved for guests. I kept my extensive gun collection in a smaller room along with numerous disguises I used when I went undercover to attempt to solve a case.

I took a long hot shower and then rinsed off with cold water to get my blood circulating. I thought about the neighborhood that I was going to that night and decided that the street hustler disguise would be most appropriate. I selected a dark gold single pleated, single breasted, three piece shark skin suit and brown silk shirt. After putting on the suit vest, I put on my twin shoulder sling holsters which held twin .44 Magnums - my weapon of choice in a gun fight. I put extra rounds in my inside suit coat pocket. I put on brown silk socks and brown alligator shoes. I selected a gold Rolex watch and a diamond encrusted pinky ring. Next, I put on a thick gold chain with a diamond and ruby encrusted Capricorn shaped medallion. I took a long wig of real human hair off of the top shelf of the closet. It made me look as though I had a long permanent hairdo which is fashionable among pimps. I put on a brown $200 Stetson and a pair of gold rimmed glasses. I looked into the full length mirror. Everything I had on was genuine and tailor-made. I looked like a successful pimp/gambler/playa.

I went to my safe inside the closet and took out $500 in hundred dollar bills. Every legitimate street hustler had to have his "bankroll" to flash. It was proof of his success. I rolled the money up and wound a thick rubber band around it. Before I left the house I put on a generous splash of Aramis cologne. I wanted to be irresistible to my quarry. Many detectives and undercover cops failed because they didn't dress, talk or conduct themselves in the exact manner as the people they were attempting to portray. The smarter criminals and hustlers always sniffed them out. Some cops had even lost their own lives attempting to infiltrate criminal organizations. That's why I went the extra mile and spent the extra money. You had to dress the part, walk the walk, and talk the talk. As a consequence, I met with great success.

On the way out the back door I grabbed my silver lion headed black cane from the umbrella/cane rack. It was actually a twelve gauge shotgun capable of firing one shell. It was activated by a hair trigger in the lion's mouth. I wanted to be ready for anything. The character that I was portraying that night was of a pimp named Clyde Caddy Walker, the Night Stalker, the Boss Talker -- meaning he had the gift of gab. Clyde was in town from New York. He was looking for some young black and white ho's (whores) to take back with him.

CHAPTER 8

I took Martin Luther King, Jr. Boulevard to the airport. When I pulled up to the booth to the airport parking garage, an old looking, and diminutive but spirited and affable white man gave me my ticket and said, "Have a nice trip, sir." His eyes were green and full of life. He seemed to be happy just to be alive. He reminded me of a leprechaun. "Thank you, sir," I said. "And you have a pleasant night." H grinned broadly and waved as I pulled off. Some people were just naturally friendly and likeable.

I walked over to the Rent-A-Car lot and had to present the clerk, a young, oversized white lady, with my driver's license and take off my wig and sunglasses before she would accept my credit card. "I'm sorry, Mr. Henry. I see in the computer that you are a frequent customer. I really thought that someone might have stolen your credit card," she said apologetically, while still puzzled by my street appearance.

Pimps and hustlers usually didn't own a credit card, and you would hardly find one renting a car. They usually sported their own tricked-out (flamboyantly accoutered) vehicles. I assured the circumspect young lady that I appreciated her precautions and explained that I as dressed in that fashion because I would be attempting a costume party called the "Player's Ball."

When I left the Rent-A-Car lot in a late model Cadillac Coup Deville, it was 7:30 p.m. I took Quebec Street to Interstate 70 and headed toward the Roundville Projects where I hoped to find Pig or some new news of him. Not everyone who lives in the projects is a crook, dope fiend or welfare recipient. Many decent, hardworking women live there with their children because the rent is at a reasonable price -- usually ten percent of the renter's income.

The women use the money saved from living in the projects to purchase other essentials, such as, food, clothing, and transportation.

However, there are many cons to living in the projects. Crime is high, and the misery index is off the charts. Other than the hardworking mothers, there are few positive role models for young girls and boys growing up there. I read in a sociology book that whenever there was an increase in unemployment, there was a corresponding increase in a majority of criminal activity. (I could have told them that.)

Not many men live in the projects; this is true for a variety of reasons. Chief among them is the high unemployment and incarceration rate among black men. According to the Urban League, there are more black men in prison than in college. Many of the black men who would normally be residing in the projects are in prison or jail -- or dead. Another factor contributing to the absence of the black male is the pain of feeling ashamed. Many of them are ashamed to be in a family that they cannot provide for.

Then you have the lazy, sorry, shiftless, no good black men who just don't give a damn. They impregnate women and girls and then leave. Some of them may come around on "check day" to sweet talk the women out of some of the money they will need to use to provide for themselves and their children. But the feeling of loneliness drives these women and young girls to give in to these poverty pimps. This is not a behavior confined to just black men. You will find these men who prey on lonely women among every race.

Multiple generations of black boys were growing up with no fathers, mentors, or positive role models. I was mentoring three boys but I was only one man. More black men needed to get involved in the raising of these children. If they did not, we would have only ourselves to blame for the tragic aftermath.

I got off of Interstate 70 onto York Street and drove the twenty blocks to the infamous Roundville Projects. Many black men, women, and children had lost their lives there -- in more ways than one. I believed in the Weed and Seed Program announced by the government decades ago. The problem was, there was too much weeding and not nearly enough seeding. When I pulled into the parking lot of the building where Pig's mother resided, there were ten to twelve young boys ranging in ages eight to eighteen, standing out in front of the building. A few girls held onto their boyfriends.

A Cadillac in that area got immediate attention. A few of the boys came forward. I stepped out of the car. "Man, you a boss playa (sophisticated street hustler with plenty of money, women, clothes, and jewelry) for real!" one of the young boys exclaimed, as he admired the late model Cadillac and the rich street attire of Clyde Caddy Walker. The boy looked to be about fifteen. "Look here, Shorty," I said. "I'm about to make a run up to Pig's Momma's crib (apartment/house) to kick bow bows (talk with her). What you charge a pimp to keep your eyes on his ride?" "Man, playa," the boy responded. "Peel a nigga' off a sawbuck (ten dollars) and you'll be straight." I pulled out my bankroll and handed him a hundred dollar bill. His eyes lit up and he grinned as if he had hit the lottery.

"What's your name, Shorty?" I asked him as I leaned against the Cadillac and placed my hands in my pocket pulling back the suit coat in such a way to let him see that I was strapped (carrying) with a pistol. "They call me Solo." The boy proudly announced as he took note of the pistol. "Look here, Solo, I want you to break the other young shorty's off a piece of that c-note. You understand me?" "I got you, playa. Don't even trip," he said. "When I come back down there, I'll break you off a c-note just for yourself if everything is straight." "Like I said playa, you ain't even got nuttin' to worry about. I'ma handle my business." Solo stated with bass and bravado.

Since we were having such a good rapport, I decided to ask Solo a few questions about Pig. "When's the last time you saw that nigga',

Pig?" Nigger was an ugly word to me, but what street hustler would have reservation about using the derogatory term? I had to stay in character in spite of my reservations. Though the word did not have the same connotation when used by blacks as it did when used by racist whites, I still found the word demeaning and self-debasing.

Solo did not hesitate before he answered.

"Man that nigga' got little (left the scene) 'bout two or three months ago. The po (Police) at his ass." "Was he still staying with his ol'-G (mother)?" I asked. "Naw, that nigga was creeping with this young bitch named Wanda and her Momma up in 4B." "I'm lookin' fo' that nigga' 'cause he supposed to be introducing me to some young ho's that want to get money up in New York. I'm 'bout to holler at his ol'-G and see if she knows where I can get at him." I gave Solo some dap (clashed fists with him) and headed up to Mrs. Chester's apartment.

I lived in the City of Denver for thirteen years before I had seen or even heard of the Roundville Projects. There were built in north Denver near some hog farms, far from the heart of the city and far from whites. The stench from the farms had been sickening. The farms are gone now, but the people remain. I had found out about the existence of the Roundville Projects when our church Sunday School bus started picking up four kids from there. There was an undeniable stigma attached to them. In our youthful, black, middle-class ignorance, we had equated poverty with abnormality. If you were poor, you were someone to be mocked and ridiculed, and woe be to the helpless young girl or boy who wore raggedy clothes or shoes to church or school. The teasing would be cruel and relentless. A lot of children don't attend school because they are ashamed of the attire they wear.

As I ascended to the third floor on the beat-up, dirty, graffiti-ridden elevator, I tried to imagine how a child felt growing up in such an environment. Did he or she blame the parents? Did they believe that they were inherently inferior to those who possessed more materially and lived under better circumstances? There was no doubt in my mind that some of the young men that were standing in front of the building were selling drugs. What other business was there in Roundville?

I stepped off the elevator conscious that I was in a different world. A world in which life was harder and cheaper. The cinder block walls were dirty and emblazoned with gang insignia. The linoleum floors were filthy. Evidently no one was making sure that the janitors did their jobs, which could only have added to the misery and frustration that the inhabitants must have felt. Or, maybe some of them had become accustomed to the way things were and no longer resisted - or cared - not even in their minds.

Pig's mother opened the door after three knocks that were made at thirty-second intervals. When she opened the door, I barely managed to conceal my shock. It was a good thing that I had sunglasses on! Mrs. Chester was exceedingly and morbidly obese. She barely stood five feet in height but must have weighed over 400 hundred pounds. She looked to be about 70-years-old. I later found out that she was only 55. She appeared to be wearing a queen-sized, sky-blue bed spread with a hole cut out for her massive head, which was ensconced in a humongous torques bath towel. Never had I seen such a head before. There were no contours to her face below her lips. Her jaw, chin, and neck were a gelatinous mass of fat. Her eyes were coal black and her skin was a sickly looking shade of yellow. If I had been a child, I think that Mrs. Chester's appearance would have frightened me to death.

"Can I help ya?" Mrs. Chester whispered in a barely audible voice. Her breathing was heavy as she looked me up and down.

"Yeah, I believe you can." I said with a broad smile which in turn elicited the same from Mrs. Chester.

"Well, come on in then. I don't know what I could do fo' ya', but a little company would be nice. I ain't had anybody been up here for months 'cept for the girl that cleans around here and the man that does my shoppin'," she said as she turned and began her arduous trek back to her sofa. Mrs. Chester's feet did not leave the floor as she shuffled along in a pair of bright pink slippers. "Close the doe' and have ya' self a seat." Mrs. Chester whispered as she neared the sofa.

In mark contrast to the hall I had just left, Mrs. Chester's apartment was very clean and fragrant. I would even describe it as immaculate. In Mrs. Chester's living room was a sofa, a loveseat, and two matching recliners. They were all of royal blue velvet with red oak armrests, frames, and legs. The sofa and the loveseat sat across from each other with a well-maintained, intricately carved red oak coffee table in between. The recliners sat facing each other on the opposite ends of the coffee table. There were matching end tables on the right of each recliner upon which sat light blue lamps with rose colored shades. The walls were rose-colored and the drapes appeared to be made from the same material as the couches and recliners. It was an attractive arrangement. Mrs. Chester plumbed down in the middle of the sofa. Her body spread to both ends taking up the whole length of the sofa. She appeared to be taller than she actually was because she was sitting on at least two feet of rump.

In the east corner of the apartment, a big forty inch flat screen color television was playing a videotaped soap opera. On Mrs. Chester's right, an assortment of chips, dips, colas, and candy was on the TV dinner tray along with a variety of inhalers and other various prescription medications. I sat on the chair to Mrs. Chester's right and said, "Mrs. Chester you must be an interior decorator. This is one of the most beautiful apartments that I have ever seen. Where did you get such lovely furniture?" Mrs. Chester's face and eyes lit up and she smiled from ear to ear as if I was about to take a picture of her. Her cheesing exposed some very good and expensive dental work. Her left front tooth was crowned with gold. "Oh thank you Mister... what is your name?"

"I'm sorry, Mrs. Chester. Please forgive me. Clyde Caddy Walker is my name and I am very pleased to meet you." I said flirtatiously. "Thank you Mr. Walker. And I'm please to meet you too." Mrs. Chester said and giggled. "I picked this here furniture out at Reggio's in downtown Denver. My son, Pig, paid $10,000, cash money. Yep, he sho' did. That boy loves his Momma." Mrs. Chester, said, with pride and emphases on the word loves.

It was obvious that someone was taking very good care of Mrs. Chester. The bill to maintain her enormous weight must have been outrageous. "Speaking of Pig, Mrs. Chester, that's why I am here. I heard that he could help me out in the line of business I'm in." I said. Mrs. Chester's face became sour and I think she got a shade darker. "I don't know where my baby is. I ain't seen him in months. Those crackers sent him to prison fo' sta-che-tory rape five years ago. When he came home, they wanted to put one of them devices on his leg so he couldn't run off. He says he won't live like that -- people always knowing where he is. He calls me and sends money from time to time, but he don't come around here no mo' because they lookin' to lock my baby up in prison again. They say that girl he was messin' with was 13-years-old. I done seen that girl myself. I don't know how many times she done ate at the table. She looked like she was nineteen or twenty. She had breasts bigger than mine."

Mrs. Chester began to wheeze; she grabbed one of her inhalers. After two shots, she seemed to have calmed down. "That's too bad, Mrs. Chester. I'm sorry to hear all that. You can't tell them young girls ages now days. I think it got somethin' to do with all them hormone shots they inject into those hogs, chickens, and cows." I said, in order to gain Mrs. Chester's confidence and trust.

"Ain't that the truth? I think that's what got me so big," she said with a chagrined smile. I wasn't going to feed into that fantasy. Mrs. Chester's weight was clearly associated with her eating. "Uh-huh," I said. "Well I was sho' hoping to touch down with him on the business tip; you don't have no idea where I might be able to find him?"

"Naw. He scared to say where he at. He thank they done bugged the phones and everything. But if he calls and you leave me a number, I'll sho' give it to him," she said with a sincere look on her face. I gave her, a number to the disposable cell phone I kept for such purposes. She wrote the number down on a black phone book that she took from a huge black purse that sat on the coffee table in front of her.

"Well, Mrs. Chester, is there anything that I can do for you before I leave?" I asked. "Well, if it wouldn't be too much trouble," she said, averting her eyes from me and looking towards the kitchen. "Can you go in the kitchen and bring me a bag of cookies off the top shelf of the cabinet to the far left, and a half gallon of ice cream out of the fridge. I'm real tired and I can't reach up on that top shelf. I done tol' that man 'bout puttin' stuff out of my reach." "It's no trouble at all, Mrs. Chester." I said standing and smiling as I headed toward the kitchen.

Her son and food, and perhaps television were her only sources of joy. With her son gone, she had only food and the television. They were taking a heavy toll on her. Her craving for food overcame any embarrassment she might have felt asking a stranger to go into her cabinets and refrigerator to bring her food that I'm sure her doctors must have told her she had no business eating.

As I walked past the east wall leading into the kitchen, a very peculiar looking photograph caught my attention. Sitting on the oak étagère was what appeared to be a photograph of black pig with a red shirt and an afro wig on. At first, I thought that someone had dressed a pig up and put a wig on him for laughs -- like the photographs of monkeys and dogs with clothes on smoking cigars and playing poker, or engaged in some other human activity, but on closer examination, I realized that the photograph was actually that of a human being. It then dawned on me that the photograph was that of Dale Chester, a.k.a. Pig. Never before had I known a nickname to so accurately describe its possessor. Pig actually resembled a pig! He had the huge head, neck, and jaws of a hog. His nostrils were so large that they hardly seemed human. He would not be difficult to find. Anyone who had seen him would remember him. I thought that his life growing up as a child must have been horrendous. I wondered what freak genetics had conspired to produce such a face. If there ever was a candidate for plastic surgery, I was looking at it!

Mrs. Chester's kitchen was very clean and modern. All of her appliances appeared to be well-maintained and fairly new. There was even a dishwasher and garbage disposal -- appliances virtually unheard of in the Projects. I opened the cabinet and brought down a package of chocolate chip cookies from the top shelf. There was an assortment of at least twelve other varieties in the cabinet. Sitting beside the refrigerator was a huge freezer. Out of curiosity I opened it. It was full of all kinds of fish, poultry and beef. I opened the refrigerator and took out a half gallon strawberry ice cream. There were a variety of six other half gallons of ice cream. "What flavor of ice cream would you like, Mrs. Chester?" I asked out of curiosity. "Clyde, bring me anything. I like 'em all!"

There had not been a fruit or vegetable in the entire kitchen. I closed the refrigerator and took Mrs. Chester her ice cream and cookies.

"Thank you," she said as she tore into the cookies. "You didn't see nothin' in there you wanted?" "Naw, but I'll give a few of those cookies a try, if you don't mind." She smiled and held the cookies out to me -- but not before putting two more into her mouth. "Won't you stay jus' for a lil' while longer, Clyde? I ain't had anybody up here to talk to in a while. The man that brings me my groceries just puts 'em up and leaves." Mrs. Chester said pathetically. I looked at the Rolex. It was 8:45 p.m.

"Yeah," I smiled. "I guess I can stay for a lil' while." Mrs. Chester blushed and went on to tell me how Pig was all she had in the World. She said that he had taken care of her since he was 12-years-old. She said that Pig's father had been an alcoholic who had been twenty years her senior. He used to beat her and Pig. He died about twenty years earlier from cirrhosis of the liver. She was the one who had named her son Pig. "He looked jus' like a lil' ol' pig the first time I saw him," she said.

In addition to her obesity, Mrs. Chester was suffering from high blood pressure, diabetes, bronchial asthma and gout. She knew that Pig sold drugs and normally went with the women he sold drugs to. She said that the drugs gave him something that women wanted (money) and made him attractive to women who otherwise would not give him the time of day. She loved her son and would do anything for him. She ate all the ice cream and cookies during the course of our conversation. At 9:30 p.m., I kissed Mrs. Chester on the cheek and told her I would be back in touch soon. She blushed like a little girl and thanked me profusely for sitting with her and listening to her troubles. I suspected that she was attempting to kill herself with food.

CHAPTER 9

When I exited Mrs. Chester's building, the drug trafficking business was in full swing. There were people coming and going. Some in cars, most on foot; they were black and white, young and old, male and female. All were chasing that elusive euphoric first high that they had experienced when they inhaled their first hit of crack or shot of heroin. That high was gone -- never to return, but the dope fiends kept chasing the dream, feeding the criminal justice system and making other people rich.

Solo was leaning against the hood of the Cadillac talking to two emaciated women -- crack addicts no doubt. When he saw me coming, he said something to them and they hurriedly walked off.

"Caddy Walker!" Solo shouted as I drew nearer.

"I told you, you was gonna be straight."

"My man Solo," I said. "You're a man of your word; I like that."

I peeled off another hundred and gave it to Solo. He seemed well-pleased. "How late that money be jumpin' like this?" I asked Solo, as I observed money and drugs being exchanged all around me.

"Man, it be poppin' like this 'til two, three in the mornin'." Solo said enthusiastically.

"You slang (sell drugs)?" I asked the young boy.

"Naw. They won't let a nigga' get down cause my Momma strung out. They think I'ma be givin' her drugs 'steada sellin' 'em. They got a nigga' on security," Solo said as he patted a small bulge under his shirt near his wallet.

I was glad I had on the shades; otherwise Solo would have seen the pain in my eyes. Where were the Churches and the Preachers, the

Masjeeds and the Imams, the Synagogues and the Rabbis? Hell, where were the police?

I remember thinking -- how could a society allow its children to be corrupted in such a manner? More good men and women need to get involved into the lives of these children. Blacks need to wake up to the reality that no one is coming to rescue them. We had better do it ourselves.

"I'm sorry to hear that 'bout your old-G, Solo. I hope she can get herself straight," I said.

"Yeah, Caddy, I been tryin' to get her to stop. But she jus' start cryin' all the time talkin' 'bout she can't quit. I was talkin' to her when you came down. I'ma give her half this money so she ain't got to trick (prostitute herself) for a few days. I'ma buy me and my lil' sister some food with the rest."

Solo was stronger than most of the grown men I knew. If some of their mothers were on drugs and she was prostituting herself to pay for them, and all their friends knew it, I had no doubt that some of them would go crazy and slit their wrists or blow their own brains out. They would not be able to live with the shame.

"Well, lil' man, I got to make a phone call then I'm goin' shoot up to Wanda's crib and see what's poppin'. You say she up in 4B?"

"Yeah, she up there," Solo responded.

But suddenly I felt exhausted. I had been up since 3:34 a.m.. I knew that a tired mind could make fatal miscalculations. I decided to call it a night, go home, get some rest, and start fresh in the morning.

"Look here, Solo. I just remembered a run I got to make before it gets too late. I'm gonna shoot through here tomorrow 'bout five or six in the evenin'. If you out and about, you can earn some mo' money, understan' me?" Solo's grin was enormous. "Man I'm always on lo' (location). Whenever you come through, I got you."

Driving southbound on York past the deserted hog farms and empty silos, I dialed Melissa's cell phone.

"Hi, Daddy," she chirped.

"Hi baby girl. What you doing?"

"I'm getting ready for bed. Me and Cindy just finished watching the Nutty Professor on DVD," she said, then laughed. "Eddie Murphy is real funny." "Yes, he is," I said. "Are you going to pick me up in the morning for school?" "Yes, baby girl, I'll be there at 7:30 a.m. sharp; you going to be ready?" "Yeah, Daddy, I'll be sitting in the window waiting for you." "Okay, honey. Give Daddy a kiss goodnight." She made a kissing sound into the phone and then laughed. "Cindy wants to talk to you," she said. "Okay, Honey. Goodnight." "Goodnight, Daddy. I'll see you in the morning."

"Hello, Cindy." "Did you find out where Pig is?" "No, but I'm pretty sure he's somewhere close to home. He's still taking care of his mother with drug money. You just can't go anywhere and set up shop. And he has a face that is easily recognizable. Therefore, he has to lay real low. And as you know, most fugitive black men attempt to hide in their own neighborhoods. I had another lead, but I suddenly got really tired and decided it would be best to head home and get some rest." "You made the right decision, Mack. Well, I'm going to let you get your rest. I'll see you in the office tomorrow," she said in a sweet voice. "Goodnight, Cindy." "Goodnight, Mack."

I turned off of York onto Thirty-Second Street and drove east. I was thinking about Melissa. She made my life worth living. Things were looking up. She seemed happier than she had been in months. I hoped that her recovery from depression would continue. I didn't want there to be any setbacks now that she was finally emerging from her constant sorrow.

I turned left on Dahlia and headed north to Thirty-Fifth Street. I was about three minutes from home. Mary J. Blige was singing "Reminisce" on KDKO. I could not help but to reminisce about my deceased wife. I thought about the time twenty-five years earlier that she was ready to fight a girl because she thought the girl had smiled and winked at me while we were dancing at a house party. She had, but if I had told Jackie that, it would only have added fuel to the fire. "What you smiling and winking at, heifer?" Jackie had suddenly asked the girl. "You better keep your eyes on who you're dancin' with. This is my man!" I smiled and laughed. Jackie was beautiful and petite and otherwise serene, but she wouldn't hesitate to stand up for herself if she thought that someone was trying to invade her territory or take something from her. Melissa had exemplified the same characteristics on more than one occasion.

I lived in the second house from the corner. When I turned into the alley and pushed the remote to open my garage, a feeling of apprehension ran over me all of a sudden. I felt that my life was in grave danger. My heart began to beat rapidly in my chest. I quickly looked left and right, behind me and in front of me before driving into the garage. As soon as I got inside of the garage, I quickly stepped out of the car with one of the .44s in my hand. My garage was not attached to my house so I would have to walk out of the garage door or the side door of the garage in order to get into my house. I decided to walk out of the garage door back into the alley. That would give me a clearer view of the entire house and the garage as I walked up the sidewalk to my back door.

I pushed the remote button and let the garage door down. I looked up and down the alley and into the backyards of the houses that were in plain view. I didn't see anyone; not even a dog. It was dark but I could clearly see that no one was waiting to ambush me from behind any of the apple and cherry trees lined on the left side of my back yard. I looked over at Melissa's swing set and under her merry-go-round; no one. The only blind spot lay in front of the garage. For precautions sake, I decided to climb my neighbor's fence on the right and come along the other side of the garage. If anyone was lying in wait for me, I would drop on them and would not hesitate to shoot them if they were armed.

I crept along the fence that divided me and my neighbor's backyard. When I got parallel to the garage I could see that no one was there. I began to think that I had spooked myself into being overly cautious because of the events that transpired that morning. I holstered my pistol and climbed the fence over into my own yard. I cut diagonally across the grass straight to the back door, which led to my kitchen and the landing to the basement. I set my cane against the door as I fumbled for the keys in the dark. I made a mental note to see about getting a system installed that would automatically switch the porch lights on after dark.

I found the key, placed it in the lock, turned the knob and stepped in. By the time my eyes got adjusted to the dark and I realized that someone was standing in the kitchen; it was too late. "All right motherfucka! Stick your muthafuckin' hands up." The dark figure shouted in a loud pitched, not quite feminine voice. "Make one fucked up move and you a dead nigga," the voice shouted further. I placed my hands in the air. "What do you want?" I asked. "If it's money, I think I can help you." "Shut the fuck up, nigga; came a swift retort. "I ask the muthafuckin' questions around here. Now, bring your punk ass on up these stairs," the voice commanded. There were stairs leading from the back door landing to the kitchen floor. I slowly ascended them while adrenaline raced through my veins. As I placed my foot on the last stair, the lights came on. If the intruder had not been carrying a long barreled .38, which was leveled at my belly, I might have laughed. Standing in front of me was a tall, ultra slim black man with a yellow woman's pantsuit on. He had on a pink blouse and a long blond wig. His dark brown face was garishly made up with purple eye shadow, rouge blush, and flaming red lipstick. He had a dark, razor bumped profile along his chin and jowls. I wondered what made him think that he was a woman. A long pair of women's blue pumps completed they gaudy ensemble.

"Yeah, muthafucka, it's me, the Chocolate Delight bitch. I know you didn't think you was goanna kill my man and get away with it. Naw muthafucka! It's gonna be repercussions for what you did to Cliffy." His voice cracked when he said Cliffy and his eyes watered. "Yeah, I know it's you in that pimp suit and wig, nigga. I watched your ass when you came home and when you left back out. I been downstairs and done seen all your little detective outfits. I see you like dressing up and playing make believe. Well, I got some shit I want you to put on before I kill your punk ass for killing Cliffy."

"He tried to kill me." I protested. "I was only defending myself. A man has a right to defend himself. What was I supposed to do, let him kill me?" Delight looked at me with intense hatred in his tear reddened eyes. Then he walked up to me, holding the pistol close to his side. He obviously had some experience holding guns on people. He didn't hold the pistol out from his body where it might be deflected by a swift blow to the arm like most amateurs do. "Didn't I tell you to shut your goddamned mouth?" Delight shouted and struck me in the face with his left fist. The blow was solid and I stumbled back a few feet.

"Nigga, you ain't got but a few more minutes to live, but before I kill you, I'm gonna have some fun with your punk ass!" Delight stated with a fiendish look on his face. "Strip! Get butt naked, nigga. Right now! And put these panties and shit on," Delight shouted as he emptied a paper bag onto the floor. A garter belt, matching pink panties and a bra and a pair of orange pumps were in front of me.

There was also an instant camera and some ropes. This Negro must be crazy, I thought. His first mistake was not killing me as soon as I walked in the door. His second mistake was not patting me down for weapons before he began his psychosexual attempt to debase me and avenge the death of his pedophile lover.

I stilled myself for what I was about to do. I had to be lightening quick and deftly accurate. Delight was standing three feet in front of me. I went into acting mode and pretended to be scared to death. "Please, don't kill me Chocolate! I'll do anything. Just don't kill me. I don't want to die. I have a daughter to raise," I said in a pleading, crying voice. As I said that, I bowed my head and dropped the cane and put my hand to my face. My hands were only a few inches from my guns. Delight laughed derisively and said, "Just as I thought. You mo' bitch than I am. I don't give a fuck about you or your muthafuckin' daughter. If the bitch were here, I'd kill her ass, too!" Those words sealed Delight's fate. Calm came over me and, quicker than quick, I had both .44 Magnums leveled at Delight's chest. He had a shocked look on his ugly face just before I stopped his heart from beating by pumping his chest full of hot lead. He screamed as he was knocked off his feet and landed between the refrigerator and the oven. The .38 he held had fallen from his hand. As I stood over him, he cursed me with his last breath. He said, "Fuck you nigga," in a man's voice. He died with his eyes open and his pumps on. He had been a silly person. He looked even sillier dead.

CHAPTER 10

I called the police and told them I shot an armed intruder. They asked me if I was sure that the intruder was dead. I told them that he couldn't get any deader. There is no coming back from a Mack Attack, I thought and laughed aloud.

I was delighted that I killed Delight, but as I waited for the police to arrive, my left hand twitched uncontrollably -- nerves. I had almost been killed twice in one day. I wondered if it might be time for me to get out of the business. Things were getting just a little too hot for a single parent with a daughter to raise. What would happen to my baby girl if I too died? I didn't even want to think about Melissa as an orphan. I decided that I would reassess things at the conclusion of the Sloane case.

I wondered how Delight had gotten in the house. I went around from room to room checking windows and doors. Nothing had been breached. When I came back into the Kitchen, I noticed some items sitting on the kitchen counter that I normally kept in the milk chute. My house was built in an era when milk was still being delivered from door-to-door, 1954. I closed the kitchen door that concealed the milk chute when it was open. It was unlatched. Delight was certainly skinny enough to have snaked his way through. I wondered why I had not considered the possibility that someone could have gained entry in that way before. Not everyone has the stomach to kill. Not even in a situation in which they would be justified in doing so, such as to save their own life.

Delight struck me as abnormally vicious. I believed him when he said that he would have killed Melissa if she had been with me. I thanked God that she had not been. I wondered what he had planned to do to me when he ordered me to strip and put on the female underwear and pumps. I wondered how his mind had gotten so depraved. It hadn't mattered to him that his lover had been the

"Lollipop Rapist" and that he had tried to murder me simply because I had brought his rape and abuse of innocent children to an end. All he wanted to do was kill the man who killed his man. You used to be able to tell what race a person was depending on the crime that they committed. That was no longer the case. Black people were now serial killers, baby rapists, and spree killers. I thought that there must have been some underlying cause that was producing such psychopathic personalities in America.

A squad car and two homicide detectives arrived on the scene at the same time. Detectives John Larse and Grant Strutters were already acquainted with me as a former cop and private investigator. They were also familiar with the Clifford Woodson case. They knew that Delight had bonded his lover out of the county jail by bribing a desk officer and that there was a warrant out for his arrest. I showed my gun license and credentials to the two squad officers, Kirkland and Brown, out of courtesy. Forensics had not yet arrived. "How did he get the drop on you, Mack?" Strutters asked. "He snaked his way through the milk chute," I said as I opened the milk chute and showed them that there was ample room for someone of Delight's slight build to slide through. "He was lying in wait for me in the dark when I came in. If he had shot on sight, I would be dead. Uncannily, I felt that some danger was afoot, but after a few precautions, I dismissed those feelings as nerves brought on by this morning's events." "Well, you're sure lucky, Mack." Strutters said. "Delight is a stone cold killer. He killed his first victim when he was just 16-years-old. Afterwards, he castrated him. He was acquitted on the grounds of temporary insanity. He told the jury that the 36-year-old victim had been molesting him since he was 13-years-old. The state's attorney didn't believe it because Delight was living with the victim at the time of the crime and had been doing so for 2 years prior to that. There was also testimony introduced at trial that the boy was already gay before meeting the victim, but the jury could not stomach a 36-year-old man and a 16-year-old boy as lovers."

"Through the years, he has been arrested numerous times for assault and prostitution. He spent three years in prison on one charge. That's where he met Clifford Woodson. They were cellmates. He was also the chief suspect in the brutal axe murder of a female impersonator -- I was assigned to the case, but we never could prove anything against him. It was rumored that he and the impersonator were rivals for the attention of a certain rich communications executive. The executive was uncooperative -- wouldn't even acknowledge that he and Delight and the female impersonator were acquainted. He was married at the time and had three kids."

I was stunned. I made coffee and opened a box of chocolate doughnuts. I was even happier that I had killed Delight after finding out what he had done to another victim. Had he prevailed, I might well be penis-less and dead. We talked until forensics arrived. They did not cart Delight off until 3:00 a.m. I was beat. I called Mr. Albright's cleaning service and let them know that I had another job for them. They said they would work day or night. They arrived in fifteen minutes. They were true to their advertisement.

I was so tired that I told the cleaning crew to lock the door on their way out. I went into the bathroom and looked in the mirror. There were bags under my sleep deprived eyes. I had promised to pick Melissa up for school. I took a hot shower, set the alarm clock and fell on my bed like a dead man. I woke up 2 hours later hollering and sweating profusely. In my nightmare, Delight had chopped Melissa up into 6 pieces. I was bound in heavy ropes that prevented me from moving anything except my head. Delight then approached me with a straight razor with which to cut off my testicles. I thanked Almighty God it was only a dream.

In about half an hour, I went back to sleep. The next thing I knew, Jackie had her hand on my cheek and was saying, "Wake up, Mack! It's time to take Melissa to school." I smiled and looked into her bright brown eyes and smiling face and said, "Okay, baby." Just then, I actually woke up and the alarm began to buzz. The dream seemed preternatural. I brushed by teeth, rinsed the Listerine, took a 3 minute shower and quickly dressed in black pants and a black shirt. I would have to get going if I was going to get Melissa to school on time. I filled my thermos with coffee that was leftover, grabbed 2 doughnuts -- one for me and one for Melissa -- and jetted out the back door. I drove east on 38th Street until I got to Monaco Parkway. The cool morning air felt refreshing as I took notice of the lush green lawns and abundant evergreen, poplar and maple trees that made the parkway such a picturesque and desirable street to live on and drive through.

It was 7:30 a.m. when I pulled in front of Cindy's house in the rented Cadillac. As she promised, Melissa was at the window watching for me. She came running out of the house with her backpack on and sporting a new hairstyle.

"Good morning, Daddy! Whose car is this?" she said smiling from ear to ear. "Good morning, baby girl! This is just a car I rented for a surveillance job. How did you like spending the night with Cindy?" "I loved it! We had a really nice time. Cindy made popcorn and braided my hair while we watched The Nutty Professor on DVD." Melissa was truly happy. I could see it in her eyes and hear it in her voice. "She did a good job, baby girl. Your hair looks beautiful," I said. Melissa grinned and said, "I know!" We both started laughing, and for a moment, I forgot all about Pig, Clifford Woodson, and Chocolate Delight. I dropped Melissa off at Smith Elementary School, where she was a 5th grade student, and headed for my office.

CHAPTER 11

I got back on Monaco Parkway and drove south until I came to Colfax Avenue and turned west. Traffic was heavy as thousands of Denverites drove themselves, or were being driven to work and school. Some of the restaurants along Colfax had been open all night. A certain section of the Avenue was known for its prostitutes, strip clubs, gay bars and nightlife. I turned into the parking lot of a Mom and Pop restaurant. I was hungry. Melissa had assumed that both of the doughnuts were for her and had eaten them. She said that she was a growing girl and that she needed a lot of food. I laughed but secretly harbored the fear of our relationship changing. Soon I would have to stop kissing her good night and calling her baby girl. I felt kind of sad about that.

An attractive white woman with blue eyes and red hair came to the table where I had taken a seat and said, "Good morning sir. May I take your order?" She was quite a knockout. Her uniform was tight in all the right places. I suspected that she knew that and used her feminine assets to increase her tips. "Yes, you may." I said. "I'll have two orders of turkey bacon, three scrambled eggs, two orders of toast and two glasses of orange juice." "Aren't you the hungry one," she purred. I felt a moment of intense longing for the young woman and then stifled it. I couldn't tell if she was just fishing for a tip or if she was actually coming on to me. But, there was no way in the world I was going to get involved with a pretty, young, white girl; or an ugly old one for that matter. Jackie would turn over three times in her grave and Cindy would probably shoot me. Melissa would say something like, "What's wrong with your, Daddy? A black woman ain't good enough for you no more?" She would have gotten that from her mother whom she had heard make that statement in regard to rich actors and athletes who had married white women after they had gotten rich. I thought about O. J. and Nichole. They had met at a restaurant.

"Yes, young lady," I said. "I am quite hungry." Then I looked her in a manner which indicated that I wanted to keep things respectable. She gave me the "I understand" look and went off to place my order. The food was delicious and service was prompt. I left Jenny -- that was her name -- a $3.00 tip. She beamed and said, "Thank you, sir. Please come again. It was a pleasure to serve you." I left thinking that Jenny's good looks and courtesy would take her far.

It was 8:45 a.m. when I arrived at the office. There was a Ward's Furniture truck parked out front. I walked to the driver's side and let the burly driver know that I was the customer for whom he had brought the new desk. I opened the front door and showed them where I wanted the desk placed. I then turned off the large, noisy fans the Albright cleaning crew had left to dry the carpet. They had done an excellent job. The stains and stench were gone. There was a faint smell of oranges and lemons in the air.

After the delivery men set the desk up, I gave both of them a $10.00 tip and thanked them. The two black men smiled in unbelief. Blacks had a reputation for being notoriously poor tippers. It wasn't true of all blacks, but in a racist society, many were always judged by the actions of a few. There's not just white on black racism, or the reverse, there is also the intra-racism practiced by many blacks. Many of us believe and perpetuate the negative stereotypes promoted by the media, rumor and innuendo. "Thank you, Mr. Henry, sir," the burly dark-skinned driver said. "We appreciate it." "You're welcome, brothers," I smiled and said in response, "Have a nice day."

It was my way of saying I appreciate you black men for working hard for a living and providing for yourselves and your families. Good black men needed all of the support that they could get. If we came together, we could get a lot accomplished.

Cynthia Alice Beasley was late. It was 9:15 a.m. After the delivery men left, I went into my office and stretched out on the sofa. I only intended to take a quick nap but I did not wake up until 11:45 a.m. When I awoke, Cindy was sitting in the chair across from me, seemingly in a trance. She was looking at me but not seeing me. She had not realized I was awake until I spoke to her. "How long have you been staring at me, woman? Can't a man rest in peace?" I said teasingly. When Cindy's eyebrows furrowed and she tilted her head to the right, I knew I had done something wrong. "Don't be playing with me, Mack Henry. You know that your behind was almost put to rest, permanently, last night!" she said angrily. I wondered what she knew about last night's events. Seeing the surprised look on my face, Cindy provided the answer. "My girlfriend, Officer Lettie Brown, called me this morning while I was getting ready for work and asked me was you all right. She said that they had been at your house until three o'clock this morning and you looked like you hadn't been to sleep in days. Said some psychopath homosexual had done broke in your house and tried to kill you. What kinda raggedy ass alarm system you got in there? How many times I got to tell you that you got enemies? What if Melissa hadn't spent the night with me?"

When she mentioned Melissa, her voice cracked. Cindy was a tough woman. She had faced death and had been willing to end life on more than one occasion. She wasn't easily rattled, but when I looked up at her after having dropped my head like a child being scolded by his mother, Cindy's eyes were watering profusely. I stood up and walked over to her. She rose to meet me. "Mack. Mack… I love you!" she said hesitantly. "Be quiet," I said as I put my arms around her waist and began to kiss her on her full, brown and red lips. The salty taste of her tears mixed with her sweet tongue was intoxicating. I squeezed her tight and dropped my hands down to her soft, round behind. She wiggled her hips, grinding herself into me and moaned. We went on like that for five minutes.

That was a close as I had come to what my mother would call fornicating in 26 years.

I had never made love to any woman other than my wife. Jackie and I had met in the summer of 1974 and been inseparable until her death. We had both grown up in religious families where "the Lord" reigned supreme and premarital sex was frowned upon. But in our adolescent reasoning, we decided to become man and wife at thirteen years of age. Jackie's best friend, Lori, conducted the ceremony. We didn't consummate "the marriage" until two years later. When Jackie's mother found out that we were sexually active through eavesdropping on one of our late night telephone conversations, we were forbidden to see or speak to each other. My parents had agreed with the banning.

We subsequently ran away from home and slept in churches and hospitals at night. During the evening, I sold candy from door-to-door for a red headed and bearded man called Big John. He would drive us to middleclass neighborhoods in Denver and its surrounding suburbs. We gave our potential customers a bogus spiel about being poor inner city youth selling candy to raise money for summer camp. I was somehow more convincing than the other boys -- probably because I actually needed the money -- and managed to sell my whole box of candy each night. Big John had even begun to give me a few extra dollars each time a new recruit needed to be trained. I had earned about $20.00 a day. That was enough to keep Jackie and I fed and our clothes washed. I gave the money to Jackie like I had observed my father give my mother money from his paycheck each week to buy groceries and clothes for her and my siblings. He then paid all of the other bills himself.

Jackie and I were happy and were scheming to find a way to enroll in another school. After two weeks, however, our parents relented and left word with Lori, whom they knew that Jackie was in frequent contact with. They said all was forgiven -- just come back home.

After seeing that we could not be separated and that we truly loved each other, they agreed to sign consent papers allowing us to be married at sixteen, with the provision that we finish school and attend church regularly. We lived in my father's house until we were eighteen.

I knew no other kind of intimate relationship. That's why, if I was going to be with Cindy, it would have to be as my friend, lover and wife. I broke our embrace and stepped back from her. "Cindy," I began as I took her soft hands into mine and looked into her lovely dark brown eyes. "You are an intelligent, courageous and beautiful woman. Any man would be blessed, fortunate and happy to have you as his mate." "But I don't want any man, Mack. Baby, I want you." Cindy interrupted. "Mack, I think that I have been in love with you since the day you interviewed me for this job. I never said anything out of respect for you, Jackie and Melissa. I was happy to see a strong black man taking care of his business with his wife and child. And I never, ever would have said anything about my feelings for you, Mack, if Jackie had not passed on. I know that you and I and Melissa can be happy together. I love that girl as if she was my own daughter, and she likes me too, Mack. Just give us a chance. Mack, you'll see. We'll be happy!"

I knew Cindy was sincere and I wasn't surprised by her words. I had known for some time that she loved me. Jackie knew it too. What impressed us, however, was her nobility and integrity. Some women would not have cared about my wife and child. In fact, more than one woman tried to seduce me away from my wife; several female clients in particular. They had not cared that I was married. Most men in my situation would have allowed themselves to be seduced. In fact, married men are often the initiators of such illicit love affairs.

"Cindy," I said. "I have always liked, admired and respected you. In recent days, I think that I have begun to love you. I don't know a woman, other than my deceased wife, who is more appealing to me than you. But, I don't think that I will ever love another woman the way that I loved, and still love, Jackie. She is attached to my soul and no one could ever take her place in my heart."

"Mack, I know how much Jackie meant to you," Cindy said. I don't want to take her place. I just want a place in your heart of my own. I have never met a couple more in love and well suited than you and Jackie were. If you could love me half as much as you loved her, that would be a mighty love and I would be happier than I have ever been in my life." She stepped to me and placed her arms around my neck and said, "Mack, I haven't been with a man in two years. I need you." Her pretty brown face was glowing and she had a serene, almost angelic look. I ran my index finger across her bottom lip. It quivered. Her nipples were hard against my chest. Little Mack - if you know what I mean - was at complete attention as Cindy grinded her hip into him.

Cindy had on a yellow silk blouse and a whit skirt that hugged her hips and behind. It took all of my powers of self-restraint to not strip her naked and make love to her like she had never been made love to before. After 26 years of experience, I knew what I was doing.

"Cindy, I want to make love to you so bad it hurts. But, I want you the right way. When I make love to you, it will be as my wife." "Is that a proposal?" Cindy asked, both happy and disappointed at the same time. "It's almost one." I grinned. I want to court you for a little while so we can get to know each other outside of the office and work context. Plus, I want to subtly broach the question with Melissa. I need to know how she would feel if I married another woman." Cindy sighed, then smiled and said, "You know you got my panties all wet!"

I couldn't do anything but smile at that remark and say, "A few more grinds from them hips and my boxers would have been in the same condition!" Cindy laughed. "Okay. It's official then. You and I are now going together. For our first date, I would like to take you to lunch. Get your things," I said. "Okay, Honey." She was calling me Honey already. "But first, I have got to freshen up and change my panties."

Women are much more prepared for emergencies than men. I don't know a man that carried an extra pair of drawers around in case of an accident -- sexual or otherwise. I had never looked into Jackie's purse or her personal belongings. In my father's house, there had been a clear demarcation line between the masculine and the feminine. My brother and I didn't even put lotion on our ashy legs because it was considered "sissified" in our house. I didn't know until that day that women carried extra pairs of panties in their purses. Or was Cindy the only one that did? I made a mental note to ask her about it at a later date.

CHAPTER 12

In memory of Almost Dead, Mr. Blair, I took Cindy to the popular Greek restaurant that he had temporarily shut down a few years earlier. I also took Cindy there because they had good food and excellent service. They were expensive too, but I wanted my girl to know that nothing was too good or expensive for her, if I could afford it. Most men will give a woman anything she wants if, he loves her and he can afford it. Women make a mistake when they try to get a man to purchase items she and he both know he can't afford.

I felt blessed that a beautiful and intelligent young woman was in love with me and my daughter. I knew that Cindy would make a good wife and mother. She had all of the requisite qualifications to hold both titles. I couldn't get a word in during lunch. Cindy went on and on about who would be attending the wedding, what I would have on, what the bridesmaids would have on, what she and Melissa would be wearing, what church we would get married in, how we would fly our parents in from out of state, how much money we would spend. I let her go on and on. I didn't want to rob her of her joy; especially after she had given up on the prospect of getting married two years earlier. She hardly touched her meal of lamb chops, mushroom soup and salad. I ate it for her.

We got back to the office at 1:30 p.m. Two potential clients had left messages on the answering machine. When Cindy returned their calls, one was looking for a missing uncle. The other wanted his wife followed because he feared that she was cheating on him. Cindy began a preliminary investigation into both cases. She would get as much information on both subjects of the investigation as possible and brief me later. If necessary, I would call Gordon Travis, the only other black private investigator in the City, and have him handle the surveillance on the wife. It usually did not take long to gather the necessary evidence to prove that a spouse was or was not cheating. Cheaters usually met at the same cheating time and the same cheating place time after time.

Meanwhile, I retired to my office to consider the known facts of the Sloane case: There were five days left before Valerie was to have the money that Pig had demanded in exchange for the tape. Pig was on the run, hiding out somewhere. There were not many places that he could conceal himself considering his unique facial features. He had to be among family or friends.

Solo had told me that Pig used to creep with a young girl named Wanda who lived in the Roundville Projects with her mother. I thought that she might hold the key to his whereabouts. If I failed to locate Pig before the deadline, I would have Valerie to meet him at the designated place while Cindy and I lay in wait somewhere near. We would then jump him and confiscate the tape from him; that is if he actually had the tape on him. If he did not have the tape with him, I would make him tell me where it was hidden. I wouldn't torture him. I never had to go that far, but I knew how to make a person think that I would mutilate them if they did not give me the information I wanted. I would then arrest Pig for violation of parole.

If possible, however, I wanted to avoid the foregoing scenario because it was potentially dangerous to the client. Pig struck me as both foul and volatile. There was no way to tell what he was actually planning to do to Valerie. He might have been planning to abduct her and re-enslave her. Maybe he intended to take the money and kill her. There was just no way of knowing what he had planned. Maybe Pig was smarter than I was giving him credit for. Maybe he was not only cold, but calculating as well. He obviously knew that Valerie would not go to the police with the videotape and the blackmail letter. He also knew that she would not go to her husband and tell him about the rapes and degradation she had been made to endure as a young girl. He knew that she was ashamed of what happened to her and she didn't want anyone else to know. If I could find Pig's hideout before the deadline, he would be more likely than not to have the tapes on him. In that case, I could confiscate the tape or tapes in a mock stick-up and later inform the police as to his whereabouts. That way, he would never know that Valerie Sloane was involved.

I called Cindy into my office and told her my thoughts about the possible whereabouts of Pig and the various scenarios I had contemplated to relieve Pig of the tapes. I wanted to see if she could provide me with some additional suggestions on the matter. She shared my belief that Pig had to be holed up somewhere in Roundville or with close friends or relatives because he would be unable to move about and shop for himself or sell drugs without being noticed and remembered. Cindy also shared the belief that it would be best if we could find Pig's hideout before the deadline, break in and confiscate the tapes and whatever money and drugs Pig might have in a mock robbery. Pig's mother told me that she and Pig had both been born in Denver and had never left the city. It was highly unlikely; therefore, that Pig could be lying low in any of the surrounding suburbs or counties. Cindy agreed that Wanda was likely the key to Pig's whereabouts.

At 2:30 p.m., I told Cindy I was going to pick up Melissa from school and take her to her grandmother's house to spend a few nights. "Why didn't you have that milk chute sealed?" Cindy asked as I was about to leave. "It never occurred to me that a grown person could fit through it," I said, somewhat annoyed. "When I accidentally left my keys in the house one day while rushing to get Melissa to school, I had put her through there so that she could unlock the back door. She barely fit. It might have occurred to me at the time that someone could use a child to gain entry into my home, but I didn't feel any pressing need to do anything about it at that particular time. And, there is no way I could have imagined that a super slim killer would slither into my home through a tiny box shaped hole." I further explained in a defensive tone of voice.

"Do you feel any pressing need, now?" Because I don't want you or Melissa living in that house until you get that taken care of, Mack!" Cindy said, as if she was the boss of me. I didn't like her talking to me like that, but she was right. I was still feeling kind of angry with myself because my daughter could have been with me when I had come home the previous night. Though I believed that I would have still been able to protect her, I would have exposed her to a sadistic killer, and that bothered me. It bothered me a lot. "Well, I won't be home until 6:30 tonight, so call Secure Alarm Company and see if they can come out to my house." "Okay, Honey. You know I'm just looking out for my man and my future stepdaughter," Cindy said to soothe my wounded ego. "I know, Baby. It's okay," I said and walked out the door.

On my way to Smith Elementary School, I called around Denver seeking information on Pig. Howard Byrd said that Pig was still at large and that so far, he wasn't a suspect in any new cases. Some of the petty criminals I received information from in exchange for money knew of Pig, but only one of them had seen him in the last three months. Shady Richard claimed that his dope fiend wife had purchased some heroin from Pig at the Roundville Projects about two months ago. He also warned me that Pig had killed before. He hadn't seen Pig actually commit the murder, but he had it from a so-called reliable source that Pig had killed a 14-year-old boy for teasing his Momma. They had found the boy in one of the Project dumpsters with his throat cut from ear to ear. If that were true, I thought, it merely confirmed my suspicion that Pig was volatile and mentally unstable. He was subject to do anything.

I then called Melissa's grandmother, Ollie Jackson, to let her know that I was bringing Melissa over to spend a few nights. She was used to me bringing Melissa over on short notice and was delighted every time I did so. She told me that even if she had plans, she would gladly cancel them to take care of Melissa. Mrs. Jackson had taken Jackie's death very hard. Melissa reminded her of Jackie and made her feel that a part of Jackie was still on earth. As a consequence, Melissa was doted on by her and greatly loved.

It was 2:58 p.m. when I pulled in front of Smith Elementary. Except for the sixth grade crossing guards who had been let out 5 minutes earlier in order to take their positions on the crosswalks, there was not a soul on the street. The brown and beige brick houses and two family apartments across the street from the school were well maintained. All the trees and flowers were in full bloom. Bees darted in and out of the various species of flowers that added beauty to the homes and neighborhood. The peaceful, nearly tranquil atmosphere belied the rumpus that would shortly erupt.

At exactly three o'clock, the school bells rang. The shrill sound was music to those kid's ears. It had been to mine, too, when I attended the same school some thirty years prior. Seconds later, hundreds of children of various sizes, shapes and shades of brown came out of the four designated exits. It was the last day of school and they were all as happy as could be. In contrast, I imagined that it was a somewhat sad day for some working parents who would now have the additional financial burden of hiring a babysitter or putting their children in a daycare while they were at work.

Watching those children screaming, laughing, running around, and darting in and out of different groups made me smile; I was struck by their innocence and uncomplicated life. I hoped that they would all transition into fine adults but, the sad reality is that too many of them were destined for the penitentiary and an early grave, especially the young black boys. Because of an array of factors, many of the children were destined to become dope fiends, robbers, thieves, murderers, prostitutes, pimps, and drug dealers. Why couldn't we, or wouldn't we, as a society stop that from happening?

That was a question that had always troubled me. Based on objective facts, one could conclude that certain people have a vested interest in the perpetuation of the criminalization of certain group and classes of people. The criminal in many respects, is an invaluable commodity. President Dwight D. Eisenhower warned Americans about the Military Industrial Complex. Perhaps we need to investigate the Prison Industrial Complex and see who is really prospering from crime. The consequences of criminal activity far outweigh any potential benefits that accrue to the criminal but Hollywood will go on glamorizing violence and criminal conduct and our children will go on being seduced and enticed.

Lost in my thought, I had not noticed Melissa standing at the passenger side door until she knocked on the window to get my attention. I looked up and she had a big beautiful grin on her face that immediately dispelled the gloom that was beginning to overshadow my mind.

"Open the door, Daddy! What's wrong with you? You daydreaming about your girlfriend, Cindy? I have been standing out here twenty seconds," she said teasingly as she looked at her watch. She was time conscious, too. I couldn't help but laugh. She had her hands on her hips and had been swiveling her head back and forth like only a black girl or woman can do.

I opened the door and said, "Girl, get your behind in this car! What's wrong with you going off on your Daddy like that?"

"I thought you were in a trance. What, Cindy got her spell on you?"

Now, I knew that girls matured faster than boys, but when she said that, I felt as though my little girl had gotten mature without me noticing it. What did she know about male and female relationships, romance and love? She certainly knew that her mother and I were in love. We had openly displayed our affection but never in an inappropriate manner. I didn't know what her mother had taught her about the birds and bees. I didn't know the types of conversations she was having with her grandmother and Cindy.

Nevertheless, Melissa was perceptive. She had obviously picked up on the burgeoning relationship between Cindy and me. More importantly, she didn't seem to mind. In fact, she seemed to be encouraging it.

"Naw, baby girl. Ain't no woman got no spell on me, I said.

"Hmmmmm, yeah, right! Whatever you say, Daddy. I see the way y'all be looking at each other." Melissa said smirking.

It occurred to me that my daughter was seeking information. She wanted to know how I felt about Cindy. She was probing. How quick they grow up, I thought.

"Do you like Cindy?" I asked.

"Yeah, Daddy. She's a good woman. She's smart. She got her own house and car. She know how to cook. Her house is clean. Plus, she know how to do hair. And, she in love with you, Daddy. I can tell by the way she's always talking about you. Your Daddy this; your Daddy that. I'm telling you, Daddy, you ought to give the girl a chance." She said sounding very mature.

I was astounded by Melissa's insight as a 10-year-old girl, but I sensed a conspiracy afoot. She sounded like Cindy's pitchwoman.

"How old are you?" I asked though I already knew the answer.

"Daddy, you know I'm 10-years-old and that I'll be eleven on September 23rd."

"Well, you sound like you about 22 going on 23." How come you know so much about boyfriends and girlfriends?"

"Mommy taught me a lot and Grandmommy and Cindy are teaching me everything a young lady needs to know," she answered smugly.

"Well, I guess they're doing a good job, but don't you grow up too fast. I don't want no boys coming around my house until you at least sixteen. I don't want to bust a cap in some young fools behind. And he better be a young fool! You understand me?"

"Daddy, you crazy!" Melissa said laughing. "I ain't even thinking about no boys."

"You better not be," I said with enough baritone to let her know that I was serious.

"Do you know what courting is?" I asked.

"That's when a boy takes a girl on dates and stuff and comes over to her house to meet her parents and watch TV," she said confidently and sat back in her seat.

"Yeah, that's right. Cindy and I are courting right now to see if we really like each other. Courting gives a couple a chance to find out things about each other that they didn't know before. You might find out some good things and you might find out some bad things. Or, you might find out good and bad things, but, at least you'll know what kind of person you are getting involved with before you get married."

"Well, I think Cindy will make a good girlfriend for you Daddy, and a good wife. You'll see." She said.

I was stunned; stunned beyond belief. She had actually said that Cindy would be a good wife for me. Now I could move full speed ahead in my relationship with Cindy. I had my daughter's approval.

As I turned left on Peoria, I had Melissa call Cindy and ask her if she had made the appointment with Security Alarm Company. She told

Melissa that the company would be at my house at five o'clock that night.

CHAPTER 13

Grandma Ollie's house was in Montebello, a mixed, middle-class suburb of Denver. It was about 10 miles northeast of Park Hill. In recent years, it had become predominately black as whites moved back to the city or further out into the boondocks.

Instead of getting on Interstate 70 and exiting on Peoria Avenue, which would have gotten us there in ten minutes, I had taken the scenic route. Driving down Montview Avenue had reminded me of the days when I used to catch the city bus to Jackie's house. I would have to walk thirteen blocks south just to get to Montview Avenue. The Montview bus, number twenty-three, would take me to Peoria Avenue. The Peoria Avenue bus ran so infrequently, that I would wind up walking all the way to 44th Street before the bus came, but seeing Jackie's lovely face made every step along the way worth it.

Now, some 28 years later, I was driving my daughter down the same streets headed for the same destination. When I pulled in front of Mrs. Jackson's house on Fifty-fifth and Xanadu, she was outside watering the small flower garden on the left side of her front porch. The two-story colonial was made of red brick and had white shutters and gutters. A small boat and camper were parked on the street.

Mrs. Jackson and her husband, Frank, had been avid campers and fishermen prior to his death from prostate cancer a few years earlier. Since then, the camper and boat had not been used. I thought that I should ask her to take Melissa and I camping sometime that summer. At 60-years-old, Mrs. Jackson had a body and face that were still turning heads. She was about 5'8", well-proportioned and in good shape.

She turned off the water and walked over to the car as Melissa and I got out. Her skin was glistening in the sun as small beads of sweat formed on her forehead. It was 80 degrees and a slight wind was blowing down from the mountains. A pair of green shorts showed off her shapely legs. A matching halter top revealed a flat stomach, toned arms and firm looking breasts. She looked good.

Melissa hugged her and kissed her on the cheek. "How's my grandbaby doing?" she asked.

"Fine," Melissa answered, smiling and hugging Mrs. Jackson tighter.

Melissa loved her grandmother almost as much as she loved me. It was a good thing. She needed a motherly figure to love. One who loved and cared about her and would give her the best advice that she could give her.

I was standing on the side of Melissa when Mrs. Jackson said, "Mack, you not going to hug and kiss your mother-in-law?"

Since Jackie's death, my visits with her mother were always awkward. She looked so much like Jackie that I was embarrassed to look at her or touch her. They were almost the same height, the same hair color - though Mrs. Jackson's was slowly turning gray - the same light brown eyes, the same nose and lips, and nearly the same tone of mahogany red skin. She had marked Jackie and Jackie had marked Melissa. At some point in all of their lives, mother and daughter could pass for identical twins. It was as if their father's DNA was missing. The only thing that I could see of me in Melissa was my height, ears and forehead. The rest belonged to Jackie and her mother.

"Hi, Mom," I said, hugging her briefly and barely touching her cheek with my lips. She looked at me and smiled. I sensed that she understood my uneasiness.

"Won't you come in for some tea, Mack?" she said.

"Yeah, Daddy, come in for some iced tea with me and Grandmommy," Melissa jumped in.

"Okay, baby girl, you convinced me." Melissa grabbed my hand and the hand of her grandmother and we walked to the front door. After we were seated at the kitchen table and had drank several glasses of sweet, cold iced tea with lemons and eaten a fresh bag of potato chips, Mrs. Jackson told us that she would be visiting her sisters in North Carolina. She had asked me if Melissa could accompany her on the trip.

"How long will you be gone?" I asked just to make conversation because there was no way I could say, no.

"For two weeks. From June 11th until June 25th," she answered.

She knew that I would not refuse her. How could I? "Yeah, that will be okay," I said and smiled.

She and Melissa looked at each other and grinned mischievously. I then realized that facial expression could also be inherited, or perhaps Jackie had imitated her mother and Melissa was imitating them both. At any rate, the resemblance among the three in physical features and mannerisms was uncanny.

Mrs. Jackson was already taking Melissa on shopping trips and spending lavishly on her. I hadn't intervened because I knew it made her feel better and eased the pain of losing Jackie, her pride and joy, and only child.

In that back of my mind, I feared that Melissa would be even more mature after spending two weeks with her grandmother and great aunts. But, it could not be helped. I couldn't hold back that hands of time. As much as I wanted Melissa to remain my sweet, innocent, little Daddy's girl, she was inevitably racing towards adolescence and young adulthood. I just hoped and prayed that we would raise her right. She certainly would not be deprived of love, but I didn't want to spoil her either.

"Melissa," I said. "I need to talk to Grandmommy about something before I go. Will you go in your mother's room and watch television for a while? It'll only take a few minutes." Melissa looked puzzled and said, "Okay, Daddy, but don't you leave before you say bye-bye to me." "I won't, sweetheart."

As Melissa headed towards Jackie's old room, which she stayed in every time she visited, Mrs. Jackson had a worried look on her face. "What's wrong, Mack?" You don't want Melissa to go with me? I debated about asking you. I just wanted to spend some time with her and have her meet her great aunts. Before answering her, I stood up and looked down the hall to make sure that Melissa had gone into her mother's room. Her curiosity sometimes got the best of her and she would eavesdrop on a conversation of she could. In her young mind, it was good detective work.

"It's not that, Mom," I said. Then I told her about the two attempts that were made on my life and some of the details of the Sloane case. She gasped several times during the course of my narration.

"Oh…, Mack; I'm just so glad you wasn't hurt. Honey, it was a blessing that Melissa had spent the night with Cindy. I don't know what I would do if I lost you and Melissa too."

Mrs. Jackson burst into silent tears then. I walked over to her, knelt down and put my arms around her shoulders and said, "Don't cry, Mom. Nothing is going to happen to us. I'll be much more careful in the future. You can believe that. But, I'm going to need you to keep Melissa for the next few days because Cindy and I are going to be very busy trying to get a lead on Pig. We may have to go undercover for a few days. I know that Melissa will be safe and well cared for with you."

"Why don't you just let her stay with me until we leave for North Carolina? That way, you'll be able to concentrate on your work and it will give me a chance to spend some quality time with her before I have to share her with my crazy ass sisters. They gonna try to take her from me as soon as we land. I can see it now."

Mrs. Jackson had spoken in a sweet, slightly pleading voice. The voice she always used on me and Jackie when she wanted Melissa to spend the night or weekend at her house. We had always complied with her requests. Nevertheless, her suggestion made sense. I loved being with my daughter but cases were frequently coming up that necessitated me being away from home at night. It hadn't been a problem when Jackie was alive. She was always there to take care of Melissa. Now that she was gone, I needed someone that I could rely on. Cindy wouldn't be able to be there all the time because she had to accompany me on jobs from time to time. Therefore, I thought it was a good idea for Melissa to get used to spending a lot of time at her grandmother's house. I also wanted Melissa to become more attached to her grandmother in the event that the worst happened and I was killed. As a father, I had to look out for the best interest of my daughter.

"That will be fine, Mom. Just don't spoil her too much. She already knows that she's a princess. You should have heard the way she was talking to me earlier. She's growing up fast."

"Oh, don't I know it," Mrs. Jackson said. "She's as mature as Jackie was at twelve or thirteen. When was that last time you saw her playing with a doll? By the way, did she tell you about the training bra?"

Good lord, I thought. What did she have to bring that up for? Didn't she know that I was embarrassed and uncomfortable discussing such issues concerning my daughter? "Yeah," I said weakly. "She told me."

Mrs. Jackson was grinning again. "You're doing a good job with her, Mack. She loves you more than anything. She's getting over the death of her mother and she seems to be well adjusted."

Hearing that from Mrs. Jackson made me feel good about the way I was raising Melissa. I wasn't sure that I knew what I was doing. Can a man really raise a woman? I did not think so. "Thanks, Mom. That means a lot coming from you."

"You're welcome, Mack. But, you don't have to raise her alone. I'm here whenever you need me."

"I know, and, I'll be relying on you more frequently in the future." She smiled and almost made me choke up because she looked so much like my wife.

"Well, I have got to get back to Park Hill. The alarm people are coming out and I need to make some preparations for tonight. You can bring Melissa over anytime to pack she has a key."

"Okay, Mack. You be careful out there. I'm going to be praying for you, Honey."

I called Melissa and told her that she would be staying with her grandmother until they left for North Carolina. I told her that I would call her and come to see her every day until they left.

"Okay, Daddy," she said gleefully as she probably imagined all the fun she would have with her grandmother. I hugged them and kissed them on their cheeks and left.

CHAPTER 14

As soon as I got onto Interstate 70, I received a frantic call from Valerie Sloane. She was certain that a man in a black Escalade had been following her for most of the day. She wanted me to come to the Denver Museum of Natural History where she had taken refuge. I told her to wait for me in the cafeteria.

It was 4:30 p.m., the museum closed at 5:00 p.m. I called Cindy and told her about the call from Valerie. Then I told her that I needed her to go to my house while the alarm company secured the milk chute.

"How do you expect us to get in, Mack? You know that I can't get all this body through no milk chute," she said sarcastically.

"I see you have jokes, huh?" I said. You'll find a set of keys under the flagstone nearest the porch. I put them there when I accidentally left my keys in the house the first time."

"Okay, Mack, but you're going to owe me big time for this one. I was getting my hair done tonight. Now, I'll have to cancel my appointment, and, there's a cancellation fee."

In my mind's eye, I could see Cindy pouting. She was vain about her hair and justifiably so. It was lovely. "What do you want in exchange for your services?" I mistakenly asked in a flirtatious voice.

"You know what I want, Big Daddy, but I'll settle for some kissing and grinding," Cindy said in a voice so seductive that made all the blood drain straight from my head.

"When I get home, you'll get all the kissing and grinding you can handle," I said and hung up the phone. Cindy would get a Negro killed thinking about her while he was supposed to be concentrating on his work.

I had no idea who was following Valerie or what their intentions were. I had to be ready for anything and, after the two attempts on my life; I wasn't playing any games or taking any chances. I checked my .45 and unlocked the glove compartment and took out the .25 automatic I had placed there earlier. It was small enough to carry in my front pocket as I walked along with my hands in my pockets and my finger on the trigger. Anyone presenting the slightest threat to my well-being would be in for a rude and violent awakening.

I got off of Interstate 70 on Colorado Boulevard. The museum was only twenty blocks away. Traffic was just beginning to pick up as Denverites and suburbanites hastened to their various destinations. I felt a surge of energy as I neared the museum. I felt like a Zulu warrior on the way to rescue a caramel colored queen from the enemy's hands. It was what I lived for. I felt good that I was able to right wrongs and deliver the abused and misused from the hands of their tormentors and oppressors.

I turned into the parking lot of the museum and immediately spotted a black Escalade. It was unoccupied and parked on the north side of the building. It was 4:48 p.m. when I reached the museum steps. I walked in and hastened to the cafeteria. It was nearly deserted. There was no sign of Valerie anywhere. I quickly began to search every exhibiting room in the museum. I found Valerie on the first floor cowering behind a huge replica of a tyrannosaur. She had on a dark pink satin dress, matching pumps and purse. When she saw me, she ran over to me and threw her arms around my waist and held me as a frightened child would do. She was trembling as I held her.

"Is he in here?" I asked her as I quickly looked in all directions.

"It's not Pig," she said in a terror stricken voice. "It's a crazy looking man with a phony limp and a fake beard and mustache. He's wearing sunglasses, a straw hat and a gray overcoat."

The description was comical. I was surprised that museum personnel had not phoned the authorities before my arrival. It was at least 80 degrees outside. Someone wearing an overcoat should have immediately aroused suspicion.

There were only four people on the floor with us. A scholarly looking old black man with spectacles on; he had white hair, white eyebrows and a white mustache and beard. There was also a black-haired white woman with two young children, who was walking away from us.

"What makes you think that his beard and his limp are phony?" I asked Valerie

"Because I stood at the door for a minute to see if he would get out and follow me into the museum. When he first got out of the car, he wasn't limping and he was walking like a much younger man. I saw him adjusting the beard as he neared the stairs. As he climbed the stairs, something about him seemed vaguely familiar. I couldn't place my mind on it, but that's when I ran and hid. I didn't want to go into the cafeteria because I was afraid he might corner me in there, and if he had come into the cafeteria, I would have screamed. I don't know if he is trying to shoot me or kidnap me or rape me, or what," she said and began sobbing.

"Look here, now, it's all right. I'm here. No one is going to do anything to you. Stop crying. It's just probably some fool who finds you attractive. I'll get him. But, what make you so sure he's following you?"

"Because, everywhere I've gone today, he was there," she said. "When I left my house this afternoon, I noticed a black Escalade behind me at several stop signs and stop lights. Whenever I turned, he turned. After I came out of the beauty shop, I didn't see him, but I saw the Escalade parked a few cars away from mine. I drove to the jewelers to pick up my husband's birthday gift and again, I saw the

Escalade in the parking lot. I looked around and saw the man I described to you peering at me through the window of a bookstore. I ran to my car and sped off. When I saw the Escalade a few cars behind me, I drove here and called you."

Her voice had calmed but she was still trembling uncontrollably. "Look, Valerie, I have given you my word, as a man that no one will harm you. I have the license plate numbers from the Escalade. We will soon find out who has been following you. In fact, I intend to confront whoever it is in this very place."

Just then I spied movement from the corner of my left eye. When I turned my head completely in that direction, a man wearing a grey overcoat and straw hat was hastening towards the north exit. Valerie saw him at the same time and clutched her arms around me. I removed myself from her clutches and told her not to move and to call 911 and an ambulance if she heard shots fired and I failed to return.

I tore out after the stalker. When he looked back and saw me gaining on him, he sprinted to the door like Jesse Owens. It was indeed a fake beard and phony limp. He couldn't have been older than me. I thought I was dealing with an amateur stalker -- maybe kidnapper or rapist -- who had selected Valerie as a target. As I ran after the stalker, I pulled out one of the .45 automatics from the holster. By the time I got to the parking lot, he was in his Escalade screeching towards Colorado Boulevard. He would be long gone by the time I got into my car and attempted to follow him. I holstered the .45 and went back inside to get Valerie. They were announcing over the P.A. system that the museum was closing.

Valerie was a nervous wreck. "Look, Valerie," I said. "I know you've been through a lot, and you're feeling vulnerable right now, but you have got to pull yourself together. You're a strong woman. If you weren't, you would have given up a long time ago and succumbed to the vices of your environment. But, you didn't, you hung in there and now, you're a shining star. The only emotion that you should be displaying is anger. You should refuse to be a victim. You have got to help me fight and capture this clown by being the extraordinary woman that you are. I promise you that no harm will come to you, but you have got to calm down. If you go home in this state, your husband is going to know that something is wrong. This must be just some chump who finds you attractive. Whoever it is though, I'm going to find out and make sure that he doesn't bother you again. Okay?"

"Do you really thing that I am extraordinary, Mr. Henry?" Valerie asked in a voice that seared my heart. Abuse often makes a child question his or her own value. Fragments from her life of abuse were still affecting her self-esteem.

"Indeed, I do, Mrs. Sloane. Indeed, I do. You are the most extraordinary woman I know. What you have managed to endure and accomplish is no less than divine," I said looking Valerie directly in the eye so that she would know I was being sincere.

"Okay, Mr. Henry, I'm going to do my best not to let this ordeal break me. You're right, I've been through worse. I fought my way out of hell to get where I am. I'll be damned if I'm going to just roll over and let someone screw me out of my life," she said with courage and resolution.

"That's my girl," I said and smiled. I was making some bold promises and I intended to honor all of them. I felt attracted toward the young woman, but not in a sexual way. I wanted to protect her like I wanted to protect my own daughter from evil plots of the evil plotters who have always preyed on the vulnerable members of humanity.

Valerie had already overcome unspeakable abuse. Forces beyond my comprehension had placed her life and honor in my hands. I would do whatever I had to do to bring tranquility back into her life. I trusted that the same forces that lead her to me would lead me to her tormentor or tormentors. I walked Valerie out to her car and sat on the passenger side as we talked. I gave her instructions on how to drive home and what I wanted her to do once she got there.

"I'm going to follow you home and drive around the neighborhood for a while to make sure that the Escalade is nowhere in sight. If you see anything suspicious, call the police first and then call me. I don't want you to take the chance of me not getting to you in time. We don't know what this joker is up to. If it's someone connected with Pig, they were probably just following you to make sure that you haven't gone to the police, or maybe they just wanted to rattle you by letting you know that you're being watched," I told Valerie as she nodded her head in agreement. I then told her about the work I had put in on the case and the gist of my conversation with Pig's mother.

"If anyone knows where he is, she does," Valerie spoke as if she were suddenly remembering Pig's mother. "He dotes on her and will do anything for her. Most of the money he made selling drugs, he gave to her. She knows what he did to me, but I don't think she liked it. But, I think she was afraid to say anything because he was all she had. She treated me nice and made sure that I had plenty to eat and went to school every day."

Valerie had a faraway look in her eyes. I knew that she was reliving the events as she spoke. Then she said, "Mr. Henry, I have a favor to ask you. I hope that it won't be imposing on your private life."

"What is it?" I asked. "If I can help in any way, I will."

"Tomorrow is my husband's birthday. We have only invited 50 guests. My husband knows of you and greatly admired your work in getting those innocent black men off of death row. He was very impressed when you solved the case of the "Lollipop Rapist" and captured that man in the process of brutalizing that young child. He would be delighted to meet you. Is there any way possible that you could attend the party? It's at 8 o'clock tomorrow night."

"I'll be there!" I said. "How could I refuse that summons of a queen? In addition, I really want to meet the illustrious brain surgeon, Alfred P. Sloane."

Valerie looked pleased and said, "Its formal attire and you can bring your wife or girlfriend." "I'm sure that my new girlfriend, Cynthia Beasley, will be delighted to come."

"Oh, I didn't know you two were lovers as well," Valerie said in a way that made me know that she counted me as a friend.

"Yeah, we just recently got together," I said, not wanting to recount the circumstances that made the way for our union.

"Well, congratulations. She really seems like a high quality woman, and she's pretty too. You're a fortunate man."

"She'll be even more delighted hearing that coming from you." Valerie laughed shyly and I went to my car feeling hopeful.

CHAPTER 15

It took us about 20 minutes to get to the Sloane mansion. It was located in Lakewood, Colorado, about 20 miles west of Denver. The Georgian styled architecture of the home was impressive. The high walls surrounding the estate were of the same golden brown stained brick as the mansion. Two imposing lions stood guard on each side of the wrought iron gates leading to the long, paved road to the mansion. Both sides of the path to the mansion were lined with identically trimmed aspens. The mansion, which had been featured in many architectural books and magazines, was a source of pride for many black Americans in and outside of Colorado. They were justifiably proud of the fact that a black family had achieved prominence and affluence through education, business acumen and intellect. The mansion symbolized the heights that any black American could achieve if he or she strove diligently to persevere, in spite of all odds to the contrary.

After the Sloane's, no mountain seemed insurmountable. I wondered if Pig was aware of the social and psychological ramifications of his threat to bring shame and scandal to this prominent, black family. I didn't think that he was.

I sat across the street until Valerie had driven inside the iron gates and closed them behind her with her remote. She managed a bright smile and waved before she drove up the path. I returned the gesture.

I drove around Lakewood for an hour in search of the black Escalade, driving past the Sloane mansion on six occasions. I was convinced that whoever the stalker was, he had not followed us and that he was not in the area.

Valerie had come a long way from Roundville. She was reaping the reward of a hardworking, virtuous woman. Pig wanted to take that away from her and send her back to a life of misery, shame and fear. I was determined not to let that happen.

At 6:20 p.m., I called Cindy and told her about the incident at the museum and let her know that I was on my way home. I also gave her the license plate number from the Escalade and told her to call her friend, Lettie Brown, and have her to call the plates in to see to whom it was registered. She told me that the alarm company had placed a bolt lock on the inside of the milk chute and that if it was opened from the outside, an alarm would be triggered. Before we hung up, she told me that she loved me and that she had a surprise waiting for me and kissed me through the phone. She was getting to me.

When I got home at 7 o'clock, Cindy was cooking barbequed steak, brown rice, collard greens and cornbread. She even had a pan of peach cobbler, which she made from scratch, baking in the oven. All of these were among my favorite foods. There were candles set at the dining room table.

Melissa obviously told Cindy what I like. I felt like the willing victim of a mighty conspiracy hatched by my daughter and Cindy. Their scheme was to get me to realize and appreciate Cindy's fine qualities and skills. Their scheme was working. If the food is as good as it smells, I had thought, the deal is sealed. What more could I ask for? The woman was fine, intelligent, she loved me and my daughter, and she might be able to cook.

Many men were sleep to the beat when it came to women, but I wasn't. Men often thought that they were acting independently when, in reality, they were doing exactly what women planned for them to do. Because of men's fragile egos, women often have to trick them into doing the right thing. After Jackie was convinced of my love, she had let me in on many secrets; secrets that she had learned from her mother and aunts. She hadn't had to be cunning in regard to me. I would give her whatever she asked me for, within reason. She had asked me for a Trans Am and, as soon as I could afford it, I bought it for her.

The appetizing aroma emanating from the kitchen drove me right into that room and into Cindy's embrace. "Hi, Honey!" she said as she hugged me and kissed me on the lips. "I thought you would be hungry after ripping and running all day. Taste this right quick." She cut off a small piece of steak that was simmering in barbeque sauce, blew on it and put it in my mouth like I was her baby. It was delicious.

"Mmmm, that's good!" I said. "I had no idea that you could cook so well."

"I do a lot of things well, Mack Henry, which you don't know about, but I am ready to reveal myself to you, entirely."

"Well, Cindy," I said. "You're doing an excellent job so far and I like what I see. Come here and let me give you that tongue you requested."

As Cindy walked the two steps to me, I took in her whole appearance. I noticed her from her curvaceous hips to her full brown and red lips. From her African nose to her cute brown toes which were painted fire engine red. I saw the golden brown curls that cascaded down her neck and shoulders. I notice her pretty brown face and the yellow summer dress that she had opened to reveal just a glimpse of cleavage.

I opened my arms and she walked into them pressing her breast against my chest and her pelvis into mine.

"Cindy," I said. "Are you sure you want to be tied down to an old man like me?"

"Yes, I'm sure, Honey," she said as she looked straight into my eyes with what I could only describe as genuine affection.

"You're only 8 years older than me. But, if you were 20 years older than me, I would still have been attracted to you. You're a good man, an excellent father, and you're handsome on top of all of that! What more could a girl ask for?"

"I just want you to be sure, Cindy. I don't want you to ever regret getting tied down with me and my daughter."

"Maybe, this will convince you," she said and then began to kiss me in a way that was quite convincing. After she got through grinding on me and everything, I did need to change my boxers. Cindy was a mess!

After I had taken a shower and Cindy and I were sitting at the table enjoying the delectable meal she prepared, Cindy's cell phone went off to "My Favorite Things" by John Coltrane. If she had gotten up and gone into the living room to answer the phone, it would have been over between us as far as the intimate aspect of our relationship was concerned. Had she gotten up, it would have indicated to me that she was already in a relationship with someone or that there were things about herself that she didn't want me to know. Either scenario was unacceptable. If I was going to be in an intimate relationship with Cindy, I had to trust her completely. I was relieved when she answered the phone without hesitation.

"Hello…," she said. "Uh huh…, uh huh… Okay…thank you, girl…All right, bye." She put the phone down and said, "That was Lettie. You will not believe who that Escalade is registered to."

"To whom?" I asked.

"Irene Chester," she announced dramatically; "Pig's mother!"

"The plot thickens," I said.

"Yeah, now we know for sure that Pig has other people helping him to pull off this caper," Cindy said.

"I wonder if his mother knows what he's up to. She must know that Valerie married Alfred Sloane. It was in the Denver Post and the Rocky Mountain News. It was also announced in "Jet" Magazine. She subscribes to all three publications. I saw them on her coffee table," I said.

"And, if Pig knew that Valerie had married Alfred Sloane, I doubt that he would keep that information from his mother or vice versa, judging by the closeness of their relationship," Cindy said.

"She claims she hasn't seen him in months, but from what Valerie says, he dotes on her. I doubt that he would let two months go by without seeing her."

"Obviously, Mrs. Chester doesn't drive. She probably had to put the Escalade in her name because Pig has never had a legitimate job. She worked as a domestic up until 10 years ago and draws disability. With a substantial down payment, she would have been able to purchase the car," I said.

"I wonder who his accomplice is." Cindy said.

""Whoever he is, he's tall and athletic. I would say no more than 34 or 40 years old."

"Maybe it's someone he met in prison," Cindy suggested. "He did serve 5 straight, right?"

"Right, and if we can locate the Escalade, I'm sure that we'll find Pig nearby. At any rate, once we find the driver, I'm sure he can be persuaded to give Pig up. In an hour, I'm heading back to Roundville to talk to Wanda and her mother. I think I'll drop in, again, on Pig's mother, too. She knows more than she is saying about his whereabouts. I don't really think she could live without knowing where he is," I said.

"Mack, Baby, Honey, Sweetheart, Big Daddy, can I come, too?" Cindy asked in her spoiled little girl's voice.

Cindy was an only child and accustomed to getting her way. I recognized it in her just as I recognized the change in my own daughter's voice and my wife's voice when they wanted to sweet-talk me into buying them something or taking them somewhere that they wanted to go. They almost always succeeded in getting their way.

"Woman, I'm going undercover as a pimp," I said.

"You'll blow my cover in that dress and hairdo!" You don't look street enough to ride with me," I said, already getting into character as Clyde Walker, the Night Stalker, the Boss Talker.

"I guess I should take that as a compliment," Cindy said. "But, in case you forgot, Mack Henry, I know how to go undercover, too. I have a mini skirt and a halter top and some stilettos that will make me look like your top money maker. I could put on a wig and I know how to make up my face to look like a prostitute."

"You do?" I said teasingly.

"Yeah, I do. And, I got your back with this."

Cindy stood up and lifted her skirt right above her thigh so that I could see the snub nosed .38 caliber pistol she had attached to her garter. I couldn't argue with that. Plus, Cindy had been undercover with be before as a crack fiend when we needed to get into a crack house where we knew a 14-year-old girl was being held hostage in lieu of $1,500 in drug money her father owed. Cindy had been quite convincing. While looking like a fiend, she had retained enough beauty to persuade the dealer into letting her do a sexual favor in exchange for 2 rocks (hits of cocaine); one for herself, and one for her man -- me. When the fool opened the door, we swooped in on him like birds of prey and rescued the girl, who was naked. She was still a virgin. We had gotten there before she was raped or tricked out of her virginity.

The police had found over $60,000 in cash in the house, along with 500 bags of crack worth $10.00 each. The dealer was serving 10 years for the crack and 20 years for aggravated kidnapping and attempted sexual assault of a minor.

We had both been happy to find and rescue the girl. Her father had gotten off of crack after that and was doing well driving a delivery truck. We received a Christmas card from him and his daughter, Crystal, every year.

"Okay, you can come with me. Just don't pull that skirt up around your thigh again, woman. I'm trying to concentrate on this case. And when I come to pick you up, you betta look just like a "ho!"

Cindy grinned in victory and said, "You'll see. I'll be lookin' like one of the finest 'hos you ever met!"

CHAPTER 16

Cindy drove home to get dressed in her prostitute disguise and I went to the basement to resume my undercover persona of Clyde Caddy Walker.

This time, I selected a "money green" single breasted, tailor made sharkskin suit along with a gold silk shirt and a gold colored fedora. I put one of my .44s in a side holster and some extra rounds in my coat pocket. I put a .45 automatic in my shoulder holster and put an extra clip in my front pocket for easy access. Drug dealers usually carry heavy fire power. If I ran into Pig, I didn't want to be outgunned.

After putting on the usual jewelry and a generous splash of Aramis cologne, I looked into the mirror. I was satisfied that I looked the part of a flamboyant, garish clothes wearing pimp. To me, it was a clown suit, but, I had to be convincing if I wasn't going to arouse the suspicion of the people I was seeking to deceive and get information from. The criminal had to totally identify with me as a criminal. I had to walk the walk and talk the talk of the criminal underworld. My life, and the life of others, depended on it.

I got into the rented Cadillac and headed to Cindy's house. I could definitely use her to enhance my disguise, I thought, and she would be dependable backup in the event that something went wrong. But, I would not let her accompany me unless she looked just like a prostitute. I didn't care if her feelings were hurt. I'd rather deal with hurt feelings than a dead girlfriend.

I pulled up in front of Cindy's house at 9:31 p.m. I was about to get out of the car to knock on her door when she emerged from the house looking sexy enough to be arrested for indecent exposure. The tight blue mini skirt she wore barely reached her thighs. If she bent forward or to one side, her assets would be seen. She had on a matching blue halter top with no bra. Her smooth, slightly rounded stomach was enough to drive a man crazy with lust and desire. Completing the get up was a blonde afro wig, fishnet stockings held up by a red garter belt and six inch red stilettos.

She sashayed down the walk swinging her hips widely from side to side. She did indeed look like my top money maker. Even a preacher would pull over and give her a ride.

"Woman, get in this car before you get us arrested for pandering and prostitution," I said, pleased by the authenticity of her disguise. She had on so much makeup that she didn't look like herself. Her face was still pretty, but a little coarser, as if she had really been in the street and seen some things.

"I told you I would make myself up to look like a prostitute," Cindy said smugly with a smirk on her pretty face as she got into the car.

"Yeah, you look just like a 'ho," I said facetiously and smiled.

"Watch it now!" she said laughing and punched me, rather hard, on the arm. "The only man that got a chance to get some of this Honey is you."

"Uh huh. Just don't let me catch you in that outfit unless we undercover or in the bedroom. Woman, I didn't know you was that thick -- good God!"

"So, you like what you see, Big Daddy?" Cindy asked in a seductive voice.

"Oh, it has gone way beyond that! But, let's get to the matter at hand before we forget that deadly seriousness of the game we're about to play. There is no telling what Pig might do if we find him and if his accomplice is with him, we might have a real gunfight on our hands," I said knowing that we were both beginning to allow our growing love and desire for each other to distract us and cloud our intellect. In such a situation as we were about to embark upon, there could not be the slightest distraction, for it could lead to a fatal misstep or a misspoken word.

"You're right, Mack," Cindy said. "We'll have plenty of time to flirt with each other later."

Then she pulled a .357 Magnum from her purse to confirm the fact that she knew that we were headed into a situation wrought with danger.

"I changed guns," she said. "Because I don't want to have to shoot somebody 5 or 6 times before they stop presenting a threat to us." She was back into full professional mode.

"I know you're sharp, Cindy. I would prefer you over any man as my back up partner." That made Cindy smile and give me a small peck on the cheek.

"So, what's the plan, Mack?" she asked, as we headed north on Monaco Parkway.

"I think that we should talk with Solo before heading up to Wanda's. I've established a good rapport with him. I think that I can get him to tell me if the black Escalade has been around without arousing his suspicion. Then we can go visit Wanda and her mother. Unless he's got some other woman or girl with him, I figure he's got to be stopping by there every now and then for some female company."

"If he's not still secretly living with them," Cindy interjected. "Because if he looks half as bad as you described his photograph to me, Mack, there just isn't too many places that he can go. You said none of your people have seen him. That means he's lying real low. He's got to be holed up somewhere in the Roundville Projects."

"You may be right," I said. "I've considered the same possibility myself. That's why we need to be extra cautious tonight. If he's still at the Roundville Projects, then he may know that Clyde Caddy

Walker is looking for him. He hasn't called me back if his mother gave him my number which indicates that he's not interested in what I'm selling or he's suspicious of me. He may just be afraid to surface under any circumstances."

"That could be," Cindy said as I got onto I-70 going west. "But it is also possible that he doesn't contact his mother that often. You said before that his mother said that he doesn't come around her because he's afraid they might get him. He may also be afraid to call her for the same reason. He might, indeed, think that the phones are bugged and he only calls her from a pay phone from time to time."

"Well, from the conversations with Solo, Wanda, and her mother, we should be able to detect whether any of them have been recent contact with Pig. If a person talks long enough, they usually begin to let subtle clues seep out unaware. We'll have to be acutely alert for that possibility. I am beginning to think that Mrs. Chester was, in fact, telling the truth when she said she hadn't seen in months. She nearly had an asthma attack when she was telling me how he didn't come around anymore."

I got off of Interstate 70 at the York Street exit and headed north. Cindy and I speculated on various aspects of the case until we arrived in front of Wanda's building at 10:05 p.m. The usual cast of characters was out and about: dope fiends, and hope fiends, dope dealers and killers, prostitutes and johns, young thugs and wannabes, and fast young girls lured by the material things that the young, and old dope dealers could buy them. When you don't have any self-esteem, you begin to measure your worth by the value of things you have on and possess.

Wrongdoing had been made fair seeming to many black youth who had been thoroughly corrupted by the unprecedented power of wealth guaranteed by the sale of illicit drugs. The fact that they were destroying themselves and their own communities was an unconsidered, and, perhaps for many of them, an unrealized factor. But, the beat goes on, there's nothing wrong. Obey your thirst. Do it 'til you're satisfied. If loving you is wrong, I don't wanna be right.

Solo spotted the white Cadillac immediately and separated himself from the group of six or seven young men who were hanging out in front of the building.

"What's up, Big Pimpin'?" Solo shouted as he gave me dap through the driver side window which I had lowered upon seeing him approaching the vehicle. He appeared to be genuinely happy to see me.

"My man, Solo. What's cracka lackin'?" I asked in my best street hustler vernacular.

"Same-o, same-o," Solo responded, meaning that the same thing that's been happening is still happening.

"Look like bidness is boomin'," I observed.

"Yeah, Caddy. These fiends and hypes cant' get enough of this shit," Solo said with a hint of disgust in his voice.

Through his lack of knowledge and being thrust into circumstances beyond his ability to control, Solo found himself compelled, by necessity, to participate in a trade that was destroying his own mother and his own community. He tried to save her from prostituting herself by working for the drug dealers as their security man. They were using him because he was a juvenile and would receive less time if convicted for carrying a concealed and unregistered weapon. He would also be the first one shot if a rival gang decided to take his turf. I wondered how long it would be before he got killed or killed someone else's child.

I admired him because he was doing his best to protect his mother. He still honored her enough to care. He was born into a bad situation and was dealing with it the best way he knew how.

"I know what you mean, lil' man," I said sympathizing with Solo in more ways than he could imagine.

"Look here," I continued. This is my main lady, Sweet Honey."

"What's up, Solo," Cindy greeted Solo in a sweet voice that was reminiscent of her *nom de guerre*.

"Ain't nothing, pretty lady," Solo said blushing.

"Look here," I said. We 'bout to make a run up to Wanda's crib--see if she done seen Pig around here. Cause I got to get back to New Yawk. You understan' me? I can't be laying around here when there's money to be made elsewhere."

"Yeah, I hear you, Caddy," Solo responded looking concerned.

I didn't have to ask him if he had seen Pig because if he had, he would have mentioned it to me when I said that I was going up to Wanda's to inquire about Pig. I could see in his face that he had taken a shine to me and was eager to assist me if he could.

I peeled off 2 one hundred dollar bills and gave them to Solo. His eyes grew large and bright and a brighter smile lit up his otherwise somber face.

"Man! Thanks Caddy! Like I said befo', you ain't even got to worry 'bout your ride. Ain't nothin' gonna happen to it while I'm on post."

"You're a good soldier, Solo" I said stepping out of the Cadillac.

"What happened to that black Escalade Pig used to have?" I asked nonchalantly.

"Man, some old mark ass nigga be drivin' it. He come through here once or twice a week with groceries and shit for Pig's Momma." A mark was someone who was square and not hip to what was happening on the street. He neither spoke the lingo of the street nor participated in the subculture of the criminal underworld.

"He be going up to Wanda's crib, too. I seen him comin' outta there befo'," Solo continued.

That was a barrage of information to process in a few moments. It was confirmation of my and Cindy's speculations. Whoever was driving the black Escalade was Pig's contact to the outside world. There was no doubt in my mind that Pig was up at Wanda's apartment. Where else could he be? Why would the man in the Escalade be going to Wanda's unless it was to see Pig? More than likely, I thought, the person who was driving the Escalade had made an appearance at Roundville the preceding day to inform Pig of the events that had transpired at the Museum of Natural History.

I hazarded a further query as to the black Escalade and its driver. "Yeah, I think I know that mark. Didn't he shoot through here about 5 or 6 yesterday? I asked Solo as I placed a mock scowl on my fact.

"Yep, that's about the time that mark came through here," Solo said as he mimicked the scowl on my face. "He hardly speak to us. He always got a wig and shit on, wearing sunglasses and shit. We woulda peeled that nigga's head a long time ago if we didn't know he was lookin' out for Pig's Momma. We know Pig got him doin' dat shit. That's why we let him come up and through here. Ain't nobody gonna mess with Pig's Momma's groceries." Solo seemed a little agitated when he mentioned Pig's Momma's groceries.

"Had Pig actually cut a boy's throat about teasing his mother because of her obesity?" Solo's expression gave credence to the possibility. At any rate, it was obvious that Pig was feared and respected in the Roundville Projects.

"Yeah, that lame owe me some scratch (money) from way back. Dig, next time you see that chump, hit me on my cell," I said as I wrote down the number to my throw away cell phone and handed it to Solo.

"You want me to hold that nigga for you, Caddy?" Solo asked eagerly.

"Naw, just let me know that the nigga on the scene and I'll be through in a gangsta lean; you know what I mean?" I said, staying in character as the Boss talker, Clyde Caddy Walker.

"Yeah, Caddy, I know what you mean," Solo said laughing.

When Cindy got out of the car, she caused a minor commotion. There was whistling and shouts of approval, lust and desire coming from all quarters. "Damn." I heard one Sweet Honey admirer say. "I'll give that bitch all my money!" In response, someone said, "Shut up you broke as nigga. You can't 'ford that bitch. That's a hundred dolla' ho. That ain't one of them crack head bitches you be messin' with."

I gritted my teeth and smiled approvingly as any peddler of human flesh would do when his top money maker was being admired. But I am not going to lie; that was my woman they was referring to with pejoratives – though they thought they were complimenting her. We were playing a dangerous game. Any crack in our cover could result in death; our own or someone else's. It wasn't secret that guns were in abundance at Roundville.

When Cindy and I reached the elevator inside Wanda's building, we both breathed a sigh of relief. We were relieved that our disguises had been believed and we were glad to get off state; for all eyes had been on us.

CHAPTER 17

When we stepped off the elevator, the pungent aroma of high grade marijuana could be smelled as it wafted through the halls. As we neared Wanda's apartment, the smell grew even stronger. Standing in front of the door left no doubt as to the source of the smell. It was coming from Wanda's apartment.

A "gangsta" rapper could be heard from the apartment rapping to a mesmerizing beat. The words were indicative of the condition of the minds of those who dwelt in the ghetto and bought into the culture of death. The rapper's refrain was "I got all kinds of honeys. And I got all kinds of lead for a nigga's head. I keep my hand on da trigga, in case I gotta bust a cap in da head of a nigga." Someone was being programmed for self-destruction. We both knew that when we got to the apartment, we would be dealing with someone high and charged up on gangsta rap. It could be a deadly combination. Therefore, we decided to go in with pistols drawn.

If we had asked for Pig, Wanda and Pig's suspicions would have been immediately aroused because no one was supposed to know that Pig was hiding out at Wanda's. Just that quick, Cindy suggested that she knock on the door and pretend to have been drawn by the smell of the marijuana. She would ask if she could purchase an ounce or at least a few joints. Cindy was clever like that. That's why I hired her.

Cindy knocked on the door and stood in front of the peephole with her hand in her purse and her finger on the trigger of her .357 Magnum. The strap of her purse was slung over her left shoulder. I stood against the wall with a .44 in one hand and a .45 in the other. When the door was opened, I would rush in front of Cindy and subdue the occupants. Cindy would cover me from the rear.

The music came to an abrupt end. "Who is it?" a young girls' voice asked through the door.

"Girl, it's Honey Sweet," Cindy said in her street walker's voice. "I smell that good ass reefer coming from yo' do' and I just wanna know if I can buy me an ounce or at least a joint or two. A bitch gotta work hard tonight and I'ma need me something to get me through." There was a moment of intense silence.

"You got two hundred dollas?" The same girl's voice asked. "Cause this is that fire bow (meaning the brand of marijuana sold on the streets as red bud).

"Yeah, I got two hundred dollas. I ain't no broke bitch." Cindy said, staying in character.

"Let that bitch in," we heard a male's voice command the girl from inside the apartment.

We braced ourselves as we heard the clicking of a lock and the sound of a chain link lock as it was slid from its groove. The door swung open with a small squeal. I quickly stepped in front of Cindy and rushed past the stunned young girl. As I reached the middle of the apartment, I surveyed all of the entrances and exits as I did so. The apartment floor was carpeted in beige. The living room was lavishly furnished with a huge brown velvet sectional couch. An expensive looking glass topped coffee table with matching end tables sat in front of the couch and on its ends. Gold colored lamps with gold shades were on top of the end tables. As with Mrs. Chester's apartment, no one would expect to find such fine furniture in such a rundown, dilapidated place. But, the drug trade had enriched many project dwellers. That's why you might see a BMW or a Lexus parked in the parking lot of a project building.

"Don't a motherfucker move! This is a stick up," I shouted as soon as I reached the middle of the floor.

Seated on the sofa in silk blue pajamas was the infamous Dale Chester, aka Pig. Seeing his hog like features in person momentarily startled me. Never in my life had I seen such a face on a human being. It was unbelievable! Had he been born a hundred and twenty years earlier, he would have been a prime candidate for the Barnum and Bailey Circus side show. He would have been billed as "Pig Boy – Half Boy, Half Pig!

Again, I imagined that life must have been extremely difficult for him as a child. Children can be unwittingly cruel. Right then, however, I could see that he had grown into a coldblooded beast. Looking into his hateful red eyes, I knew that people feared and hated him and he hated them. He was well over 6 feet tall and weighted at least 300 pounds. Even though I had a .44 Magnum leveled at his chest, I could sense that he wanted to try me. He was like an animal suddenly trapped in a cage. "Whatever you're thinkin' punk, don't even try it or else you'll visit the morgue this very night," I said in a vicious voice.

Cindy closed the door and ordered the girl to have a seat on the sofa with Pig. She had on a red night gown. Her left eye was blackened and swollen. She couldn't have been more than 15-years-old. Her black hair was braided into skinny cornrows and hung down her shoulders and back. Beneath her bruises was a pretty face. Her brown eyes were sad.

"Keep your gun on 'em while I search the rest of the 'partment, Sweet Honey," I commanded Cindy.

"I got 'em Clyde," Cindy assured me as she pulled the trigger back on the .357 and walked over and stood 3 feet to the left of Pig and aimed the gun at his massive head.

Besides the well equipped kitchen and living room, there were 2 bedrooms and a bathroom in the apartment. I quickly searched through each to determine if anyone else was in the apartment. After I was satisfied that we were alone, I backed into the master bedroom to make a cursory inspection of the videotape selection that I went through the room the first time. All but 2 of the tapes had the title of a well-known mover on it. I put one of the unmarked tapes into the VCR and was taken aback at what I saw. As a father, I almost cried. The tape was shot in the other room of the apartment. I recognized its furnishings. I had also observed several video cameras and stands in the room. Pig was shown on the tape fondling the bare chest of a young girl that hadn't reached puberty. I fast forwarded the tape to where he put his penis in the terrified looking girl's mouth. I wanted to go into the living room and blow his brains out. The other tape showed Pig doing the same thing to another girl with one addition; he sodomized her. She had been crying on the tape. I couldn't hear her crying because there was no sound, but I could see the tears dripping from her panic stricken face. I was boiling over with rage. I thought that God would forgive me if I killed Pig in cold blood, but, I knew it would bother me later. I took several deep breaths. I had to get control of my emotions. If I didn't, I would murder Pig and deal with the guilt of killing him later. It was, by far, the hardest thing I had ever done.

I told myself that the evidence on the tape was enough to send Pig away for life. He wouldn't be able to hurt another young girl. I told myself to be content with that, but I still wanted to kill him in spite of myself.

The police and the Department of Children and Family Services would come to Roundville and find the young girls and get them the psychological treatment that they needed and have them removed from the custody of their mothers, whom I suspected were unfit. Probably dope fiends that Pig was paying to abuse their daughters. He was doing the same thing to them that he had done to Valerie, only these girls looked younger than 10; the bastard. I would make sure that he couldn't do it to another child, even though it meant blowing my cover. I put the tape into my pockets and went back into the living room. Pig had begun to sweat profusely. His silk pajamas were darkened around the neck and armpits.

"Wha, wha, wha chu want man?" Pig asked thinking that I was a stick up man.

"I got over one hundred thousan' dollas in here. Jus' let us go and you can have it all – the bow, the crack and the blows (heroin). Jus' let us go!" Pig pleaded in a surprisingly high pitched whining voice.

"If you don't tell me everything I want to know, the only place your child molesting ass is going is to hell. You understand me, punk ass motherfucker?" I said trying my best to restrain myself from beating this nigga to death.

"Yeah, yeah, man! I'll tell you anything you want to know. Jus' don't kill me." Pig said anxiously.

I utterly detested Pig. I didn't even want to look at him. I just wanted to rid the world of him. But, I still did not have the scandalous videotape. I still had a professional job to do. I pulled myself together and said, "You began to molest and rape a little girl named Valerie when she was 10-years-old. She used to live with you and your mother in these very projects. Her mother was strung out on heroin. You used her addiction and moral weakness to have your way with her daughter. You raped and molested this young girl until her mother died and she escaped from your sick ass. But, you videotaped one of your rape sessions and when you found out that Valerie was doing well and was married to a prominent physician, you decided to blackmail her with the tape. I have sworn not to let you ruin this woman's life by humiliating her and her husband and family. Now, I am only going to ask where the tape is one time and only one time. If you don't tell me what I want to know immediately, I'm going to stab both of your eyes out. Then, I'm going to cut your penis off and put it in the garbage where it belongs. Do you understand me?"

"Yeah, man! I'll tell you whatever you want to know. You ain't got to do none of that. I ain't gonna lie to you. I'm gonna tell you whatever you want to know!" Pig said rapidly as sweat poured from his head and body. He was drenched in sweat. He was a pathetic coward when the table had turned.

I had not the intention of stabbing Pig's eyes out, and I certainly was not going to cut his penis off. But, if a man believed that you would, he would tell you whatever you want to know. There was not a crime he would not confess to, even if he had not done it. It was brutal racist tactic that was used in the past by racist white cops up north and down south to get phony confessions out of black men. I was now using the tactic in the cause of justice and black womanhood. I had no qualms about using this method on such a terrible brute who spat on black womanhood and abused black girls, Pig was, himself, the worst kind of racist, for he was a self-hating black man who had no reservations about corrupting and destroying black people.

"Honey Sweet," I said to Cindy. "Bring me a steak knife and butcher knife from the kitchen"

"With pleasure, Clyde," she said as she went into the kitchen.

Pig's eyes nearly bugged out of his head, as he tried to gulp back the lump in his throat.

"Now," I said in a voice so terrifying that it scared me. "Where is the tape?"

"I swear to you I ain't got it, but I know who do. I sold it to him for $50,000!" Pig said, gasping for breath and scared half to death. I knew that Pig wasn't lying, but his startling revelation greatly complicated the case and added an element of mystery and intrigue. Who could afford to pay $50,000 for a pornographic rape tape? Was it one of Sloane's enemies? How would they even know that such a tape existed? Was it one of Valerie's enemies? She had sworn that she knew no one who wanted to hurt her besides Pig.

"Who in the hell could afford to give you $50,000 for a tape of you raping a woman?" I asked in the same vicious voice as Cindy came back into the living room and dropped a steak knife and a meat cleaver on the coffee table.

CHAPTER 18

What Pig said next actually shocked me. It was an unexpected twist in the case that neither Cindy nor I would ever have imagined.

"David Sloane gave me the money for the tape." Pig said hoping that I would believe him as he nervously glanced at the meat cleaver and steak knife lying on the table.

David Sloane was the younger brother of Alfred P. Sloane. He wasn't a doctor or lawyer, but he was a well-known, if not flamboyant, banker and businessman in Denver and its greater metropolitan area. David also ran the family's 80 year old mortuary business. "Located in three convenient locations throughout the city" as the advertisement on KDKO went.

Though Sloane's banking empire consisted of just two medium sized banks located in the predominantly black neighborhoods of Park Hill and Montbello, he also had a real estate company and owned two of the largest car lots in the city. One of the commercials that ran frequently began with a sad looking family of blacks standing outside a rundown looking house. The verbiage said, "Have you been evicted from your last home? Do you need a loan? Then don't moan and groan, come to David Sloane; he won't do you wrong." The commercial ended with David standing outside his bank at the Holly Shopping Center in Park Hill and grinning and shaking hands with a line of grateful looking Negroes. I said Negroes because that is the best term I can use to describe them. There was just too much grinning and rejoicing on the part of the loan recipients. It was as if they had been slaves of Master Sloane. One big, black woman, and I mean black in the beautiful sense of the word, was heard in the background saying "Hallelujah, thank God for David Sloane!" I always thought that his cheesy bank commercials aimed at the struggling, black middle class were crass and demeaning.

"How did Sloane know that you had the tape in the first place?" I asked. "He didn't." Pig responded. "About seven or eight months ago he came up to see me while I was doing time in Canyon City prison. He told me that Valerie was a rotten, lowdown bitch and that she had tricked his brother into marrying her. He said that he tried to make his brother see that Valerie wasn't no good but his brother didn't believe him. He said he hired a private detective to investigate Valerie because he didn't believe her story about her mother and father being killed in a car accident. He said that the private detective found out that Valerie was listed as livin' at my Momma's apartment in Roundville when she went to elementary and high school. He asked me if I knew anything bad about her. That's when I told him about the videotape. He got all happy and shit and said he would give me $50,000 cash money for the tape. He said that was just the proof he needed to convince his brother that Valerie was a no good ho! I didn't trus' him so I didn't sell him the tape 'til I got out of Canyon City and he brought me the money in cash."

Pig's whole pajama suit was soaked by that time and his hands were trembling. I knew that he was telling the truth. "So who is the chump that's been following Valerie in your black Escalade and bringing groceries to your mother?" I asked.

"That's him. That's David Sloane. He said it would be best for him to use my car 'cause he needs to follow Valerie around and make sure she don't go to the cops. He say she know all his cars. Since I wasn't driving it, I agreed to let him use it. The police is looking for me so I can't be out there in the street. He said he would shop for my Momma and me. Yeah, David been helping me to lay low and he was going to help me and my Momma move to Belize."

So, Pig wasn't calculating after all. He was a dummy. Sloane was using Pig's car so that everything would fall back on Pig. Pig was being set up and didn't realize it. That's why Sloane was using the disguise. He hadn't wanted anything to be traced back to him. I hadn't pieced everything together then, but I strongly suspected that David Sloane was intending to kill Valerie and leave evidence which would implicate Pig for the murder.

"Give me Sloane's address and number." I ordered Pig.

"I don't know where he live but I got the number," Pig said as he took a card from the wallet that had been laying on the coffee table along with four joints and at least an ounce of unrolled marijuana. "I never called him though. He say only contact him in emergencies. He come by here two or three times a week to drop off groceries and inform me on what's happenin' wit' the blackmail money. He gonna give me another $50,000 after he sell the tape to Valerie."

Another set up that Pig couldn't see. He must have thought that David Sloane was being generous offering to give him an additional $50,000 after he had already given him $50,000. No, he was just keeping Pig pacified until he could accomplish his purpose. I suspected that David wanted Pig to be found with the blackmail money which he knew would probably be traced back to Valerie's bank in the process of investigating her death. David Sloane was a schemer. Pig must have thought I was serious about cutting off his penis because he just kept on talking.

"After he gets the money, he said he goin' to his brother with the tape and show him what kinda lyin' ho Valerie really is. He say he just scaring her by threatenin' to send the tape to the news and shit. He say he wouldn't embarrass his brother and family like that. But he say the bitch shouldn't have been tellin' everybody she was a virgin when she knew she wasn't." Pig said looking scared, stupid and pleased all at the same time. He seemed to derive pleasure from bad mouthing Valerie.

"So he doesn't know Valerie performed those acts under duress?" I asked. Pig looked puzzled by the question so I rephrased it. "So, David Sloane doesn't know you forced Valerie to have sex with you by threatening to kill her mother and withholding her mother's daily fix of heroin? You knew that as a child, she couldn't stand to see her mother going through the pain and sickness of withdrawal. You knew that a child would do anything she could to stop her mother from being hurt. You exploited and corrupted the bond between mother and child."

I stopped talking for a few seconds to consider the fact that Pig probably didn't understand a damned thing that I was saying. Pig was incapable of feeling shame. Fear, yes, but not shame. He had no morals. He followed his low desires wherever they might take him. He would do anything to save his own miserable life so that he could continue to inflict misery on others.

"Answer the question!" I shouted.

"No, he didn't know that! He thinks she liked it."

You told him that she liked it, didn't you?" I asked as I brought my gun back up to his chest.

"Yeah, man, I tol' him that! I was mad at the bitch for leaving me and my momma. I treated that bitch good! I bought her clothes and let her go to school. She would not have been a nurse if it hadn't been for me." Pig said with the nerve to have a hurt expression on his face.

He sounded like a cruel slave master who beat and raped his female slaves but expected them to be grateful for the food, water and clothes he gave them. I could no longer contain my rage.

"You are indeed one sick motherfucker. You rape and molest a child from the time she is 10-years-old and then have the unmitigated audacity to be offended because she had sense and courage enough to escape from your sick, psychopathic ass! "I oughta blow yo' motherfucking brains out right now!"

"Don't do it Caddy!" He ain't worth it," Cindy said sensing I was about to commit murder in cold blood. I took several deep breaths and struggled to recompose myself. After a few minutes, I looked at Pig and said, "I got some good news for you and some bad news. The good news is that I'm not going to blow your stinking brains out. The bad news is that you will be spending the rest of your miserable life in prison for what you did to these two girls on these tapes." I took the tapes out and showed them to Pig. All of the fear left his face and was replaced by pure hate. It was palpable. I could feel it seething from every pore of his massive body. He wanted to kill me.

"Yeah, I know you want to kill me, Punk! Go ahead, make a dope fiend move. Nothing on earth would bring me greater pleasure than blowing the top of your head off in self-defense." I said tauntingly. I really did want him to make a dope fiend move. But, Pig just sat there breathing hard, like a bull enraged and inflated by hate. Then the girl Wanda spoke.

"Is you sure he ain't gonna get back outta prison?" She spoke in a soft whisper. I suspected that it was Pig who had swollen her cheek and blackened her eye.

"I'm sure, sweetheart. You won't have to worry about ever seeing him again in life. When he gets out of prison, it will be in a coffin."

"He been beating me and holding me hostage for the last five months. My momma strung out on drugs too. He said if I tried to leave, he would kill me and her. I know where them two girls on them tapes live. They's sistahs; they momma strung out too."

Damn, I thought. These drugs are inflicting more misery and destruction than any racist hater of black people ever could hope to do. Somewhere, someone was laughing with glee that blacks were destroying themselves in such dramatic fashion.

"I wish you would just kill this ugly motherfucker!" Wanda suddenly screamed and burst out crying. Before Cindy or I could react, Wanda was picking up the meat cleaver from the table and violently swung it at Pig's head. He brought up his left hand to ward off the blow. The tips of three of his fingers fell to the floor as Wanda brought the meat cleaver down with all her strength and hatred.

Pig then reached under the sofa and pulled out a submachine gun. I didn't have a clear shot of him because Wanda stood frozen by fear directly in front of him. But, Cindy could see him clearly. I heard the blast from her .357 as blood poured out of Pig's mouth from the impact of the six slugs that ripped into his chest, neck and stomach. Pig went down hard, crashing onto the glass topped coffee table and shattering it into a thousand pieces. He briefly struggled to get up then collapsed heavily onto the beige carpet. I was glad that Pig was dead. Somehow, he might have escaped justice. They might have let him go someday and there was no doubt in my mind that he would return to his abominable deeds.

Wanda was laughing hysterically and pointing her finger at Pig saying, "Now your pig ass is dead! Your pig ass is dead! You can't hurt me no mo'! Your pig ass is dead! You can't kill my momma! You can't rape no mo' little girls! Your pig ass is dead! Your pig ass is dead!" Cindy walked up behind Wanda and took the meat cleaver out of her hand. The girl turned and buried her head in Cindy's bosom crying.

"Where are the money and the drugs?" I asked Wanda. I wanted to let her cry, but we didn't have a moment to waste. I didn't know if the police had been summoned or not. "It's under the couch." She answered, still sobbing. I turned the couch over. Under it were five stacks of hundred dollar bills. There was another $57,000 in bills of various denominations. Also, under the couch were 20 ounces of marijuana, 27 bags of heroin.

After Cindy helped me count the money, I gave Wanda $20,000 in hundred dollar bills and told her to move away from Roundville and do her best to help her mother get off the drugs. It was a long shot, but I still believed in the power of redemption. Maybe she would get herself together, maybe she wouldn't; it would be her choice. We also gave Wanda our numbers to call if she needed anything.

"Take the money and hide it in your room." I told her. "We're going to have to call the police and tell them what happened and what Pig has been doing. Don't worry; you won't be in any trouble. My fiancé and I are private investigators. We're licensed to carry these weapons. We'll let the police know that you defended yourself when Pig tried to use you as a shield."

"Oh, thank you, Mister! Thank you so much!" Wanda said leaving Cindy and running over to me and hugging me tightly around the waist. It was as if I had freed her. I felt good about liberating her from her tormentor and giving her and her mother a chance for a new start in life.

I left $7,000 with the drugs for the police. There was no way in hell I was going to leave them all the money. I would do my own social engineering with it. The police confiscate millions of dollars in drug money and possessions bought by drug money from the black community. None of it, however, makes it back to the black victims. I intended to divide the rest of the money between Pig's momma, Solo, and the two girls on the videotape. Wanda and the girls were Pig's victims. The deserved his money – no matter how ill-gotten. And, in many ways, I saw Mrs. Chester as a victim as well. She was a victim of cruel circumstances. I disliked what she allowed to be done to Valerie. In her warped mind, being totally dependent on her son for support and survival, she had twisted her own motherly instincts and allowed the child to be raped. I couldn't forgive her for that, but I wouldn't want to sentence her to a life of poverty and destitution either. Now that Pig was dead, she would need some money to take care of herself.

I would encourage Solo to use the money to move his mother out of the dope and gang infested Roundville Projects into a better neighborhood. If his mother didn't get herself together, it didn't matter where she lived. But I hoped that a different environment and some start-up money would give her a chance. Solo and his little sister certainly deserved a chance. It was possible that Solo would feed her the money bit-by-bit to keep her from walking the street. Her life was in her own hands. I was doing all that I could. The rest was up to her and God.

CHAPTER 19

Cindy called 911 and informed them of the apprehension and death of the fugitive known as Dale Chester. Four Denver Police and two detectives arrived an hour after that. There was no rush; Pig was dead.

The police were happy to confiscate the drugs, money and weapons. It turned out that Pig had a small arsenal of submachine guns, shotguns and automatic pistols in the apartment under a cabinet below the kitchen sink. Wanda had to lead them to the weapons. The detectives and police officers were shocked by the tape of the two girls. Two of the officers went to their apartment to remove them from the custody of their mother. The girls were found in the apartment alone and without any food. One of them needed medical attention. Their names were Bell and Crystal.

One of the remaining black police officers was unable to keep her eyes off of Cindy. When he asked her for her phone number, she looked in my direction and said, "I already got a man." The chagrined officer then walked off and pretended to busy himself with the crime scene. Cindy and I were hardly questioned. We told the lead detectives that we had received an anonymous tip that the fugitive, Dale Chester, was hiding out in the Roundville Projects making pornographic videos of children. We were also informed that he was holding a young girl hostage in 4B.

"Why didn't you report this information to the proper authorities, Henry?" David Crosby, the senior detective asked, staring at me through abnormally small green eyes.

"I wasn't sure the information I received was correct. Like I said, it was an anonymous tip. I didn't want to send you guys out here on a wild goose chase. In addition, I had reason to believe that if uninformed officers made an appearance at the Roundville Projects, particularly in front of this building, that Pig would be alerted by contacts outside the building using cell phones. He would then move his operation to another location before he could be apprehended. If the information was true, and the girl was, in fact, being held hostage, we felt that we needed to move immediately. Therefore, Mrs. Beasley and I donned these disguises and pretended to be interested in drugs. When we attempted to take Dale Chester into custody, he tried to grab the young girl and use her as a shield. He was foiled in his attempt when the girl picked up a meat cleaver that had inexplicably been lying on the table. She turned around and chopped Dale Chester in the hand with the same. Mrs. Beasley was then able to shoot him before he let loose with the submachine gun which he had secretly hidden under the sofa.' I said returning the intensity of Crosby's gaze.

Crosby knew of me and my cracking of several murder and rape cases the Denver Police had been unable to solve. Most officers I came in contact with appreciated me and all gave me all of the help I requested. Their main objective was to get the criminal off the street. On the other hand, there was a small minority of officers who resented me and hated my success. I was making them look bad, so I was told. Crosby's assessment of me lie somewhere between these two extremes.

"Uh-huh, I see. Well, Henry, I think we have all we need," Crosby said averting his eye from me to his brown loafers. "I have your number, Beasley, if any further questions should arise," Crosby concluded, unable to find any reason to detain us further. A citizen was still allowed to make a citizen's arrest and to use deadly force to save innocent lives. Moreover, both of or weapons were registered and we had a license to carry them concealed. Crosby had manifested his half distain for us by refusing to address either of us with the title of Mister of Mrs. We didn't give a damn though; he could go to hell.

When Cindy and I got downstairs and walked out of the building, the sidewalks, parking lots and streets were deserted. No one wanted to be questioned or arrested for any of the various crimes that continuously occurred on a daily basis at the Roundville Projects. Everyone was gone, except that is, for Solo. When I opened the door to let Cindy in, Solo rose up from the back seat smiling and said, "I told you Caddy, you ain't got to worry 'bout nothing. I'm always on post!"

Cindy and I both nearly fell out laughing. Solo was a man of his word. He had risked being questioned and, possibly arrested for that pistol he carried just to keep his word to me. Well his loyalty did not go unrewarded. I explained to him who Cindy and I really were. He did not seem the least bit perturbed and said, "I had a feelin' about you." I gave him the $5,000 that night and told him to come by my office in a few days. I was going to help him get an apartment in Park Hill. I cannot explain or describe how happy he was.

On the way home, I didn't need to comfort Cindy about killing Pig. In her mind, and in mine, Pig was subhuman. He was like a devil in human guise. Killing him was akin to ridding the community of a deadly virus. Pig's unchecked lusts had driven him to insanity. He had only gotten sicker in prison where little help or therapy is offered or mandated for the criminal sexual offender. But, I could read in Cindy's eyes that the brutality that Wanda and the two prepubescent girls had been subjected to deeply disturbed her.

"Bell and Crystal are free now, Cindy," I said in an attempt to get Cindy to dwell on the fact that Pig would no longer be abusing them with impunity. "Thanks to you, they will get all the help they need."

"I know, Mack. But, I can't help but think that those babies are going to be scarred for life. They have been sexualized at such a young age. How could their mothers turn them over to that brute?"

"They weren't in their right minds, Cindy. When your body is craving for those drugs it is like you become insane and will do anything to get rid of the pain. In that weak, vulnerable state some people will sell their souls. An addiction doesn't have any morals, maternal instincts or self-respect. It just wants to be fed. Look at the sisters who have lain down with dogs for crack. After years of degradation and abuse, some women give up and begin to view humiliation and abuse as a normal part of life. Pig was able to take advantage of this fact to satisfy his increasingly deviant desires," I said as I sped along Interstate 70 at over 90 miles per hour.

"Then they should give their babies up," Cindy countered. The children should not be made to suffer because the parents are addicted."

"Baby, you're speaking from your rational, sober mind," I said. "These sisters strung out on these drugs are no longer rational. That's why good neighbors, family and friends have to be vigilant and on the lookout for neglect and abuse. Also, the government agencies charged with the responsibility of guarding and protecting at risk children have to do a better job at vetting out unfit parents. But, the bottom line is this; black people must stop selling and consuming drugs. That is the bottom line!" I said, tried and exhausted.

"You're right, Honey. I'll be one happy woman when black people wake up and stop fulfilling the negative expectations of those who hate us and seek our ruin," Cindy said with a sad expression her face.

Cindy wasn't the least bit prejudice, but she was a proud, black woman. She has a portrait of Nzinga, Queen of Matamba (Angola), who had, with the help of her fierce female warriors, kept the Portuguese at bay during most of her reign, hanging on the wall behind her desk. We drove the rest of the way to Cindy's house in silence. We were sleepy, exhausted and irritable.

I escorted Cindy to her front door, holding her hand as we walked along the way. After she opened the door, she asked me to step in for a moment. When I stepped in, she closed the door and said, "I didn't want to give you this outside." She put her arms around my neck, her lips on mine and her tongue into my mouth. I closed my eyes and allowed myself to be soothed by her lovely form. While we were in that state, I decided that I would buy Cindy an engagement ring as soon as possible. I couldn't take her to her bedroom because of the commitment I made to be a good role model for my daughter. I didn't want her to give herself to any man that she wasn't married to. Therefore, I couldn't be a hypocrite by enjoining a certain moral code on my daughter but neglecting to practice the same code myself. Melissa might give herself to someone before she was married, but she wouldn't learn it from me.

I reluctantly stepped back from Cindy's embrace and smiled into her lovely brown face and said, "I love you Cynthia Alice Beasley." An angelic glow came over Cindy's face, and she said, "Oh, Mack, Honey, you don't know how long I have been waiting for this day. You are the only man, besides my father, who has ever said those words to me." Cindy started crying. "I love you too, Mack and I can't wait to fully express my love for you," she said as she hugged me and kissed me on the lips again.

"I can't wait either," I said. "It won't be much longer, though. We'll be together in that way soon enough. I'll have a surprise when I see you again."

"I can't wait, Mack! Tell me now!" Cindy said pressing herself up against me, as if to intimidate me into revealing the surprise.

"Get off me!" I ain't telling you nothing. You'll just have to wait and see Mrs. Beasley. Besides, tomorrow is already upon us. Its 4 o'clock in the morning," I said as I looked at my watch.

Cindy poked out her lips and tried to pretend that she was mad. I ignored her and said, "I was supposed to go to church this morning with Melissa and her grandmother. But, there is no way I can make it. If I went, I would fall asleep during the pastor's sermon. That would not look good, especially if I start snoring, as I occasionally do. I have to get some sleep. You should do the same. We're invited to a birthday party for Dr. Sloane tonight at 8 o'clock at the Sloane mansion. Formal attire is required."

"What? Why didn't you tell me before, Mack?" I might have wanted to get my hair done or something," Cindy said frowning.

"Well, I wasn't sure that I wanted you tagging along with me to the Sloane's. I would not want to embarrass me and you around all of those rich Negroes," I said facetiously, for I had no reason to believe that the Sloane's or their friends were snobbish. In fact, I had every reason to belief the exact opposite, when it came to Dr. Sloane, at least. He had donated millions of dollars to black organizations and colleges. Scores of black children were attending college on scholarships provided by his foundation. He was personally mentoring a few children who wanted to follow his lead into neurosurgery. I had read that in a profile done on him by a popular black magazine.

"Oh, I see. I can accompany you on dangerous missions dressed as a prostitute and dope fiend, but I'm not good enough to accompany you to a formal birthday party. Mack, don't make me get an ugly face up in here," Cindy said, jesting along with me.

"It wouldn't take long," I said laughing.

"Chump, you want to leave here in one piece? Cindy said, placing her hands on her lovely hips. "Say something else crazy and see what happens."

"I don't want no trouble, Big Cindy," I said laughing. "What I do want to know, though is, do you possess the fine attire of a lady? You've already proven that you know how to look like a prostitute; how you looking in that department?"

"You just have yourself here by 7 o'clock tonight and you'll see what kind of lady-like attire I possess, Mister. I can stand with the best of them, Honey." Cindy said snapping her fingers; "From Oprah on down!"

"I'll see you then at 7 o'clock. And don't forget I have a surprise for you -- something special."

"Oh, I won't be forgetting, Buster. It just better be something that's worth me waiting for, or else I'm going to have a surprise for you," Cindy said, taking off her stilettos and placing her hand back on those lovely hips.

"I think that you'll be delighted," I said. "And, without further ado, I bid you farewell, my lovely lady."

I got home in about 10 minutes. Normally, it would have taken me 15, but because the streets were empty, I drove home unimpeded by anything.

I called Mrs. Jackson at 4:35. I knew that she would be asleep, but I had to wake her up. They would be expecting me, otherwise, and I fully intended to be fast asleep in the next 30 minutes. I quickly explained to her that the essential details of what had occurred since I last saw her. I let her know that I was just getting home and I was exhausted! She said that she understood, told me to be careful, and said that she would smooth things over with Melissa. I thanked her and hung up the phone.

I set the alarm clock for 1:00 p.m. and promptly fell asleep with all of my clothes on. I hadn't even taken off my pistols off.

CHAPTER 20

The long hours I put in on the Sloane case and the psychological trauma of recent events finally caught up with me that day, for despite the alarm clock going off at 1:00 p.m., I did not wake until 2:47 p.m. Again, I was not awakened by the alarm clock but by the nightmare I was having.

I was bound from the neck to feet in heavy iron chains. Melissa was being hacked to pieces by Chocolate Delight, who wielded a bloody hatchet. He came toward me and said, "You thought you had killed the Chocolate Delight, bitch, motherfucker! When I get through with this lil' bitch, I'm gonna chop your ass up next."

If I hadn't awakened up at that precise moment, I believe that I would have had a heart attack. The dream was so real that I didn't know I was dreaming until I woke up. I lie in my bed for 10 minutes thinking of various methods, strategies, and tactics that I would use to prevent a dream like that from ever coming true. I would be much more protective of Melissa from then on. What I didn't know was that the dream was actually a premonition of things to come, albeit with a different villain and victim.

I got up and shaved and showered. I put on a tan shirt and tan khakis and a pair of brown lizard skinned shoes. My father had taught me to dress well on all occasions. "You never get a second chance to make a first impression," he said.

I intended to go to a jewelry store located in Buckingham Square Mall in Westminster, a suburb south of Denver. I was going there to select and purchase an engagement ring for Cindy. I estimated that her ring finger was a size eight. Jackie's had been a seven and Cindy's hands were slightly larger than hers.

I had known my deceased wife's hands intimately. Every line on her palms, the shape of her nails and fingers, the pattern of her fingerprints and the soft mahogany skin that always smelled of peach scented lotion. Whenever and wherever we sat together, I would always take her hand or hands into my own and lightly stroke and caress them; weaving my fingers in and out of hers. I did that in church, at home, at the movies, when we were out to dinner. It didn't matter. "You know you have a hand fetish, don't you?" Jackie had once said to me. "Do you want me to stop?" I asked, somewhat embarrassed. "No, Mack; it feels good." I still missed my baby and I guessed that I always would. I wondered if I would develop the same pattern with Cindy.

I drove to the mall analyzing the case all along the way of the 25 minute trip. Pig was dead. His left hand had been brutally mutilated by one of his victims and his vital organs had been destroyed by the .357 caliber bullets pumped into his torso by Cindy. His death had been most fitting and proper. "As you have done, so shall it be done unto you," was the scripture that entered my thoughts in regards to Pig's celebrated demise. He had brutally killed the spirit, dignity and self-respect in I don't know how many girls and women. He had mutilated and maimed them psychologically. He deserved everything he got. No one would mourn his death, except Mrs. Chester.

Shockingly, David Sloane turned out to be the mastermind behind a modern day Cain and Able type of plot to destroy his brother's image and humiliate and possibly kill his brother's wife. I suspected that David Sloane wanted more than just to reveal Valerie's past to her husband. I believed that his intentions all along were to expose the tape to the public in order to embarrass and humiliate his brother. Valerie would be destroyed in the process, but I believed that the real target all along had been his brother. Otherwise, why the elaborate hoax? Why ask for blackmail money? Why didn't he just take the tape to his brother and expose Valerie for the no good woman he assumed her to be? Why follow her around in Pig's

SUV? Why maintain contact with Pig? It all pointed in one direction. Sloane intended to kill Pig and possibly Valerie, and blame Pig for the murder. It also occurred to me that he might be planning to set his own brother up for the murder of Valerie Sloane.

Sibling rivalry is a most potent and deadly poison. Dr. Sloane was a successful and handsome brain surgeon. In fact, he was world renown. He had great prestige and honor in both the black and white communities and all communities in between. By virtue of being the eldest son, he had inherited the family's large estate in Lakewood, and, to top it all off, he was married to the most beautiful woman in Colorado and perhaps, the country. Objectively speaking, I had never seen a woman more beautiful than Valerie Sloane.

David Sloane probably thought that he would never achieve his brother's social and professional status. Instead of being proud of his brother and happy for his success, he was jealous, envious and angry. If you can find a motive, you can find a criminal. I thought it would be difficult to get the tape or tapes from David Sloane, but I labored in my mind for a way to do it. I even thought of abducting Sloane and threatening him with death if he didn't reveal the whereabouts of the tape or tapes. All that a man has will he give to save his own skin. I thought of burglarizing his home and searching for the tape. That would be easier to do, but were the tapes at his house? Was he storing them in a safe deposit box or storage facility? I just had no way of knowing and time was running out.

If I would secure the tapes; all David could do is make allegations. There would be no proof of Valerie's alleged promiscuity. David would not have the tape to put on the Internet to humiliate and embarrass Valerie and Dr. Sloane. Even if Dr. Sloane believed David, at least he would not have to see his wife being gone into by another man. At least the family wouldn't be scandalized by the tape.

Once I secured the tape or tapes, I would try to convince David that Valerie deserved a chance. I would tell him how Pig had lied to him. I would tell him that Valerie was actually being raped on the tape. That she only submitted to Pig under duress and the threat of death to her and her mother. I would tell him what Pig had done to Wanda, Bell and Crystal. I would pretend not to know of his plot to kill Pig and possibly his own sister-in-law. I would try to get him to empathize with the little girl whose childhood was taken away by a veritable monster. I would try to get him to see that it wasn't her fault. I hoped my plan would work. It all depended on Sloane's humanity and rationality. If he was irrational, nothing I said would affect his lust to destroy Valerie and humiliate his brother.

I called Cindy and told her to see if she could get David Sloane's address from her friend, Lettie Brown. I had already tried the phone book; it wasn't listed. I suspected that David Sloane would be at the party attempting to gage the degree of misery and fear he had inflicted on Valerie with his threats of exposure and demand for money. If he lived close to his brother in Lakewood, I would take my tools and break in his house and search for the tapes while David was attending the party. If he lived far from his brother, Cindy and I would either arrive late or leave early. I had to get those tapes. If I couldn't find the tapes in his home, I would lie in wait for him that very night, abduct him, phone Ziglioni, and see what Sloane would do when he became a potential victim.

There was only one person on duty at the small jewelry store at the mall. She was a good looking, chocolate covered black woman with snow white hair. I don't know how old she was, but there was not a line on her makeup-less face. "Can I help you sir?" she chimed as I crossed the threshold into the store.

"Yes, ma'am; you most certainly can. I'm looking for a diamond engagement ring in the $10,000 range." The woman smiled broadly in anticipation of a five to ten percent commission she would get from the sale of the ring and said, "I'm Beverly Hudson," and extended her jewelry laden, chocolate covered hand. "Please, call me Bev."

"Okay, Bev," I said allowing her to take my hand. "I'm Mack Henry but you may call me Mack."

"All righty, Mack," she said grinning like the Cheshire cat and still holding my hand. "If you'll just step over here, I am sure you will be well pleased with our selection in the price range you mentioned."

Beverly was very affable, flirtatious and polite. I left the store a half hour later with a beautiful gold and diamond ring. The total cost was $11,500.57. Driving home, I smiled in anticipation of the happy expression that would be on Cindy's face when I proposed to her and presented her with the ring. I had paid a little more than expected, but, I thought that Cindy was well worth the extra money. She would repay me in more ways than one. I could hardly wait for our honeymoon night.

CHAPTER 21

On my way home my fatherly instincts told me that I'd better phone Melissa if I didn't want to be the object of her wrath. She wouldn't call me if she knew that I was investigating a case. She had learned that from her mother, who said to her, "Daddy needs to concentrate on what he's doing or else he could get hurt. He'll call us just as soon as he gets a chance."

"Hello," Melissa answered the phone in her happy voice.

"Hi, Baby Girl." I was glad that she was in good spirits. "How's my little princess today?"

"I'm fine Daddy. How are you? How are things going with the case? Is Cindy with you?"

"Hold on girl! One question at a time. I'm doing fine. The case is coming along well and Cindy is not with me."

"Oh, I thought she was because she ain't answer her phone." I allowed Melissa to say ain't when speaking to me and the family, but she knew the proper way to express herself. I wasn't concerned about Cindy not answering her phone. I knew that no fool had run up on her. She was always prepared to handle her business with the utmost degree of deadliness, if necessary.

"She's not?" I said.

"Nope!"

"Well, she's probably tired. We didn't get in until 4 o'clock this morning. We were on a stakeout." I didn't tell her that Cindy had shot and killed a man. She was still too young for that.

"I know, Grandmommy told me. That's why you couldn't come to church with us this morning."

"How was church?" I asked.

"Oh, it was nice, Daddy. The choir sung some good songs. The people were shouting and everything." Her grandmother had taken her to Bethesda Baptist Church in Commerce Town. The choir had a reputation for turning the place out.

"What did Pastor Harrell preach about?" I asked.

"He was talking about the three Hebrew boys that were thrown in a fire (fiery) furnace. Shadrach, Meshach and Abindigo (Abednego)."

"Oh, I see. What happened when they thrown into the fiery furnace?"

"God sent an angel to save them so the fire didn't even burn them, Daddy!" she said excitedly.

"Praise God," I said.

"You coming over here for Sunday dinner, Daddy?" Me and Grandmommy made your favorite kind of chicken (fried and dipped in barbeque sauce), greens, brown rice, cornbread and German Chocolate cake?" I hadn't intended to go over there for dinner but I knew that Mrs. Jackson and Melissa would be sorely disappointed if I did not. Especially after they had prepared some of my favorite foods; women love to watch men eat and praise their food. I couldn't disappoint my daughter twice in one day. "Yeah, Honey, I'm coming. You know I wouldn't miss your cooking for anything in the world. I'll be there in about 30 minutes."

"Okay, Daddy. I'll be waiting for you. Bye."

"Bye, baby girl."

Melissa could really cook. As I said, she loved to imitate her mother. Mrs. Jackson had taught Jackie to cook and Jackie had taught Melissa. At nearly 11-years-old, she could prepare a full course meal all by herself.

I was about five minutes from Cindy's but I decided not to stop by there. I suspected that she was in the process of getting gorgeous for the party. I didn't want to interrupt her with my presence. I called her instead. She answered the phone on the fourth ring.

"Hello."

"What's up baby doll? I thought I'd give you a call," I said.

"Hey, Mack, it's you. What's going on? You coming over?"

"Naw. I ain't coming over there. And what do you mean, 'it's you?' Who else could it or would it be. You not stepping out on me already are you?" I asked jokingly but in a serious tone of voice.

"Don't start no stuff with me, Mack Henry. You know that I'm not even thinking about no other man. I got the man I want."

"That's right," I said. "Just make sure you keep it that way."

Cindy laughed and said, "You crazy. Why aren't you coming over, though?"

"I'm on my way over to Mrs. Jackson's house. She and Melissa cooked one of my favorite dinners and invited me over for Sunday dinner. You know I couldn't refuse. I had already disappointed them by not attending church."

"Uh-huh, I see. Well, what time you coming to pick me up?" Cindy asked with a slight degree of stress in her voice. After 28 years of being with a woman, I was keenly aware of subtle mood changes. I perceived that Cindy didn't think that Mrs. Jackson should be cooking no meals for her man. That was her job now. Women could be extremely territorial; even when they weren't trying to be.

"Didn't you tell me to be over there by 7:00?" I asked.

"I'm just making sure that nothing has changed. You know I've been running around all day getting ready for this birthday party. You really should have told me earlier, Mack." Cindy protested. "You have no idea what I had to go through to get Latrece to do my hair on Sunday. The girl charged me double the price, and double the tip that I normally give her. Then I had to go out and get some new shoes to go with my gown." Cindy said exasperatedly.

I knew that she was partly upset because I wasn't coming over and that I was on my way to another woman's house for dinner, but still, she had a point. When a woman is right, she was right. An intelligent man knows not to gainsay her when she's right. Being an intelligent man myself, I did the intelligent thing by apologizing. I said, "I'm sorry, Honey. You're absolutely right. I should have told you the moment that Valerie invited us. I appreciate everything that you did to ready yourself for the party. I know that you have gone through a lot of trouble. I promise not to do it again. I'm sorry, Honey Sweet."

There were a few moments of silence before Cindy spoke. She really wasn't through berating me, but I had cut her short by apologizing.

"Well, okay, but if you do this again, Mack Henry, there are going to be consequences."

"Oh, I'm scaaaaaared, Big Cindy. I'm scaaaaaared," I said in a feigned frightened voice.

"You better be scared, buster, if you know what's good for you," Cindy said in her tough voice.

"Oh, so you think you can take me down?" I asked.

"Yeah! I think I can take you down and you are going to find out that I can take you down the next time you pull a stunt like this."

Cindy sounded so serious that I stared laughing. Cindy laughed too.

"Before I let you go, Cindy, I need to tell you what Valerie Sloane said about you when I told her that you were my girlfriend yesterday."

"What did she say, Mack? What did she say?" She asked all eager to know.

"She said that you were pretty and you were a high quality woman."

"Really! Mack, she said that?" Cindy asked incredulously.

"Yeah, baby, she really said that. You know stars recognize stars," I said.

"She's a sweet girl, Mack. I really hope that we can help her," Cindy said.

"I do too, Honey. I do too. Speaking of which, was Lettie able to get David Sloane's address? I asked.

"I'm waiting for her to call me back now, but she didn't think it would be a problem.

"I'm thinking that we can drive by there tonight and see if we can get in there to look for the tape or tapes. I'm bringing my tools."

"Okay, Honey," Cindy said. If she doesn't call me back within an hour, I'll call her again. Is there anything else that you need me to do?"

"Nope. I just want you to know that I miss you."

"You miss me? Really, Mack?"

"Yeah! Your lips, your hips, everything."

"I miss you too, Honey. Hurry up and get over here so that I can look at you."

"Look at me? All right; I'll see you at 7:00. I love you, Mack."

"I love you too, Cindy."

"Bye, Mack."

CHAPTER 22

Since I had already showered and shaved and only had to put my black tuxedo on, I calculated that I had approximately one hour to spend with Melissa and her grandmother before I would have to leave.

The meal was superb and I enjoyed the pleasure of being catered to and fussed over by my daughter and mother-in-law. There is no replacement for family life. A lot of men are missing out on tremendous happiness by trying to stay single.

Melissa and Mrs. Jackson looked more like mother and daughter than grandmother and granddaughter. I was thankful for Mrs. Jackson. She added a dimension to Melissa's personality that would otherwise be missing.

Melissa was a little sad when I had to leave so soon, but I promised to come back the next day and take her to Lakeside Amusement Park. Jackie and I had gone there every summer since 1978 and we had taken Melissa there every year since she was one. We had hundreds of photographs of Melissa riding on miniature trains, horses and planes.

I got home at 6:25. I had 20 minutes to get dressed and 15 minutes to make it to Cindy's house. I would easily manage it. I brushed off my tux, selected a crisp white French cuffed, dress shirt, a maroon bowtie and pocket square and a pair of black, patent leather shoes. I put on a splash of Polo cologne and took my onyx and platinum cuff links out of Jackie's jewelry box. She had kept them there so that she could find them when she got ready to dress me. She had been telling me what to wear since we were thirteen. I went along with it. She had excellent taste, but I was quite capable of dressing myself. Just then, I heard her voice echoing in my ear, "Wear your blue jean suit tomorrow to school and a red shirt. I'm going to wear mine and a red blouse." She had said. I smiled. I was happy to remember those small things about her.

I hadn't worn my onyx cuffs since I had flown Jackie to see "Othello" on Broadway and to one of the most posh and expensive restaurants in New York, Picasso's, on our 25th wedding anniversary. Jackie had been ravishingly beautiful that night in her dark pink, velvet gown, sheer red silk stockings and cherry red, high heeled pumps. The ruby and diamond necklace with the matching earrings and bracelet that I had given her for our anniversary complimented her skin tone and attire very well. Her hair had been pulled back and held into place by pearl studded combs and bobby pins and fell in a cascade of curls at the back of her head like a waterfall. She was so beautiful that night that I wanted to see her like that all the time.

The next day, I persuaded her to put on the same attire and have a portrait done. I said I persuaded her because she was extremely modest and acutely shy about her beauty. I had to insist. The artist truly captured her beauty. In a portrait, she looked like a mahogany queen. Whenever I looked at her portrait, which hung in our living room, I was still mesmerized by her lovely, bright, brown eyes, flawless skin and well-formed lips. When Cindy and I got married, I would have to remove the portrait and place it in Melissa's room or take it over to Mrs. Jackson's. Cindy didn't need a visual reminder that she had a rival for my love and affection.

I got into the Cadillac and realized that I had left Cindy's ring on my dresser. I went back and retrieved it. With all she had been through, she deserved to know that our relationship was secure. I didn't think that I could say it better than with the ring. I kept the price tag on it to save her the trouble and expense of having it appraised. Women just have to know certain things. Cindy would benefit greatly from the knowledge and experience I had gained from my long life and relationship with Jackie.

I got back into the car and headed for Cindy's house. I had opted for a slender, 9mm pistol, which I wore clipped to my waistband at the small of my back. It was surprisingly comfortable there and most importantly for that night's event, undetectable.

I pulled up at Cindy's at exactly 6:59. I had on a platinum Rolex, Jackie's 25th wedding anniversary gift to me. I was walking up the flagstone walk to Cindy's front door when a forty something year old, brown headed, white woman, who was trimming her hedges, gave me the most flattering compliments that I had ever received. She said, "Mister, I don't know who you are, but you are quite handsome and dashing in that tuxedo. Denzel Washington and Billy D. Williams don't have a thing on you!"

I'm not vain either, but I felt that compliment and grinned like there was no tomorrow and said, "Well, thank you, Madam. You are quite good looking yourself."

She wasn't quite good looking, but she was pretty enough and her body was still shapely. You could tell she was doing some type of exercise frequently. She blushed and I kept walking straight into Cindy's house. By the time, she had already opened the door and, from the look on her face, was about to cuss somebody out. I circumvented her by immediately beginning to extol her beauty which, at the time, was truly extraordinary. Cindy's honey-brown skin was more radiant than I had ever seen it. Her full African lips had been painted the color of ripe juicy plums and looked just succulent. I resisted the urge to suck them into my mouth. Her light brown hair was highlighted with streaks of gold and pulled up into a four inch, golden ring with flowers in high relief. Long, soft curls swirled around her ears and neck. She had on a strapless cream colored gown. It was heavily embroidered with gold flowers around the waist. It was split about six inches above her right knee exposing well-formed calves and ankles that were beautified by the straps of the cream colored satin pumps adorning her pretty feet. She wore a gold choker with matching diamond shaped earrings which hung nearly to her shoulder. She had a single half inch gold bracelet on her left wrist. The smell of her designer perfume was sensuous and intoxicating. I looked at her longingly and admiringly and said, "The Goddess Isis herself would have been envious of your radiant beauty. You are exquisitely fine, beautiful and lovely. I am extremely proud to have someone as lovely as you to escort to the party." Cindy blushed and then, the largest grin I had ever seen came over her face, revealing healthy pink gums and pearl white teeth.

"You are absolutely stunning," I said. "Now, I am afraid to take you around all those rich and influential men that will be at the party. They might try to seduce you away from me!"

"If the sexiest man on earth had Bill Gates' money, he couldn't seduce me away from you, Big Daddy," she said convincingly. "I love you, Mack, and you are the only man I want, and, the only man I need."

"We'll see," I said as I stepped to her and kissed her on her lovely, long neck. I did not want to mess up her makeup and I did not want her lipstick on my lips – not even for a second. My father had so traumatized my brother and I with fear of becoming "sissies" that to this day, I refuse to put lotion on my legs – no matter how ashy they might be. No lipstick will ever touch my lips, I thought. I knew my phobia was purely psychological, but I couldn't depart from it. I had never gone undercover as a female and I never would.

For a few seconds I debated about asking Cindy to marry me before we returned from the party and whatever might unfold. But, I didn't want her giddy with excitement and distracted in her mind. We both had to be mentally acute that night. Something might happen when we saw David Sloane at the party, or, we might be in for a surprise when we attempted to break into his house. Something might unfold unexpectedly, I thought. And the last thing I wanted was for Cindy or me to be hurt because we were distracted by our feelings for each other.

But just as quickly reason stepped in and I realized that I was being chauvinistic. I wasn't all that. Cindy wasn't going to lose her mind and stop thinking just because I asked her to marry me. I took Cindy's hand and got down on one knee. Tears immediately began to run down her cheeks ruining her makeup. I'd better make this quick, I thought. "Cindy," I began as I took the ring out of my pocket. "I did not think that it was possible for me to love another woman as I have come to realize that I love you. You are sweet, sensitive and intelligent, and lovely in all kinds of ways. I need you each and every day of my life. Would you do me the honor and grant me the privilege of being my wife?" Cindy got down on her knees and said, "Mack, today you have made me the happiest woman in the world. I feel like God has finally answered my prayers and blessed me with the man of my dreams. Yes, Mack. I will do you the honor and grant you the privilege of being your wife." I put the ring on Cindy's finger and she gasped. "Oh, my God Mack! It's beautiful! It must have cost you a fortune," Cindy said as her eyes twinkled from the light of the diamond. Then she kissed me on the lips and all of my phobias disappeared. I would have been too psychologically awkward for me to turn away from her lips and say, "I don't want your lipstick on my lips."

The potency and urgency of the moment had been too strong for phobias. We kissed and embraced for a few minutes before I disengaged my lips from hers and said, "Are you ready to go?"

"Yes, Honey. I'm ready. Just let me redo my makeup and get my purse and wrap. It won't take me five minutes," Cindy said as she smiled angelically and rose from the floor.

"Are you strapped?" I asked. Meaning, are you packing a pistol.

"You know I am," she said. "You just want to see these big juicy thighs. You ain't slick." We both started laughing. She was partly right but I told her that her word was good enough for me. I didn't want to get distracted by her lovely flesh.

When Cindy went into her bedroom, I took out my white handkerchief and vigorously rubbed my lips. Nothing. Jackie hadn't worn lipstick, but just some kind of gloss. Apparently they had made some new advances in non-smear makeup that I had been totally unaware of. It was a good thing.

Cindy reemerged 10 minutes later looking as beautiful as ever. She had put on a matching wrap and was holding a matching purse. She was truly lovely and I told her so again. I opened both doors for her and we headed towards our date with destiny as Cindy kept looking down at her ring.

CHAPTER 23

"Did you get David Sloane's address?" I suddenly remembered to ask Cindy then wondered why I hadn't asked her earlier. I was the one giddy with excitement so it seemed because I kept on thinking about how fine Cindy was and what we would be doing on our honeymoon. Realizing that I was tripping, I focused my attention on the matter at hand.

"Yeah," she said as we drove south on Monaco Parkway. "I have it right here in my purse. He lives in Lakewood as well. Lettie said that you owe her dinner."

"See when she's available and make reservations at Denny's." Cindy burst out laughing and said, "I hope you know that will be dinner for three. No woman is going to dinner alone with my man!"

"I know, but seriously, make reservations at one of the downtown restaurants. Tell Lettie she's welcome to bring a guest. It's our treat. Now what's the address to David Sloane's place?" According to the map, David Sloane lived about two miles from his brother on Columbine Lane.

"Do you think we should have told Valerie that David is the one behind the blackmail scheme?" Cindy asked.

"I don't think so. I debated it in my mind. He's not ready to spring his trap yet, so she's not in any physical danger. He wants her to go through the ordeal of withdrawing $100,000 from what is probably a joint bank account. He's diabolical. He likes to see his perceived foes suffer. But I also thought that I might be able to convince him to abandon his scheme and seek some professional help for his jealousy and insecurity. I'm hoping that I can get him to abandon his scheme by making him aware of the fact that Valerie was raped and threatened with death to herself and her mother if she didn't do what Pig ordered her to do. I didn't want to tell her that it was her own brother-in-law unless I had to. Imagine how frightened she would be." I said.

"Yeah, I can imagine that," Cindy said. "Poor girl, she is really a lovely person - inside and out. It's a shame she has to go through all this mess after all she's been through already. Should we tell her that Pig is dead? That might make her a little happier and relieve some of her stress."

"Yeah, but she's going to want to know if we found the tapes. If you get a chance to talk to her alone tell her that he's dead and that we have a pretty good idea where the tapes are and that we believe we will have them in our possession soon." I said.

It was a quarter to eight when we arrived in Lakewood. I decided to find David Sloane's house before we went to the party. That way I could go straight there from Alfred and Valerie's mansion, and wouldn't have to waste any time searching for the place. Following the map, we found David Sloane's residence in about 5 minutes. It was only a 4 minute drive from the Sloane mansion.

"Since we're already here Mack, let's break in now. David is probably already at his brother's party." Cindy suggested. She really wanted to bring Valerie some good news.

"What if it takes us awhile to find the tapes?" I asked.

"Then we will be fashionably late, Honey. I'm sure everyone is not going to arrive exactly at 8 o'clock." Cindy's suggestion made sense, so I went along with it. I had learned long ago to respect the intuition and insight of a woman.

The private road to David Sloane's residence was unlit, though lamp posts could be seen evenly spaced along the way. The shrouded in pitch black darkness a veritable forest encircled the home and kept out any light from the street lamps on the public road. I shut off my headlights in case someone was still at the mansion, like a housekeeper or gardener. I had to drive along at a snail's pace as we strained our eyes to negotiate the road. I drove up to the attached six car garage and got out with my burglary tools. I had learned the trade from a master, Cat Burglar Bob, who had got religion and quit the trade. He wasn't religious enough; however, to return the money and jewelry he had stolen from his victims.

The house was fairly modern and reminiscent of a French Château. Parked in his garage was a late model BMW and an antique Rolls Royce, and Pig's black Escalade. When I flashed the penlight around the Escalade to check the plates, I saw something that raised the hairs on my neck and let me know that there would be no dealing with David Sloane, for he was a veritable psychopath.

The object lying on the ground on the side of the back left wheel was unmistakable. I tried the garage door. It was locked. I examined the door closely. It didn't appear to be connected to an alarm system, so I picked the lock and slowly turned the knob. No alarms went off but I couldn't be sure that a silent alarm had not gone off somewhere and that the Lakewood Police weren't on their way. When I went into the garage, I flashed the penlight around the frame of the door until I was satisfied that it wasn't connected to an alarm.

I went over and picked up and examined the object that had me alarmed. It was Mrs. Chester's bright pink slipper. Though fairly new looking, the foam rubber heels had been compressed to the flatness of a quarter under the pressure of her tremendous weight. She was the only one who could link David Sloane to Dale Chester, the pedophile/rapist/drug dealer and would-be blackmailer. Sloane must have found out that Pig was dead and panicked. Mrs. Chester probably called him in a fit and told him of her son's death. Perhaps she had blamed him for Pig's death, thus, unwittingly summoning her own executioner.

There was no doubt in my mind that Mrs. Chester was dead. If she were alive her house shoe would have been on her foot and not in my hand. I went and tried the door to the house. It was locked. There was no alarm on that door either. I wasn't surprised, though. Some rich people never thought they would be robbed. I'm sure that the criminal population in Lakewood is very low, but thieves drive too. Nevertheless, I was glad that David Sloane had not considered the possibility that a thief might break into his house. I still would have gotten in; it just would have taken longer for me to dismantle the alarm. I tried several picks before I was able to unlock the door. I had never come across a lock like that before. It seemed ancient. Like the lock to a medieval castle. I was glad I had made Cindy wait in the car; she probably would have had something slick to say about me taking so long to pick the lock.

When I turned the knob and entered the house there wasn't a sound to be heard. The garage floor had led into the kitchen. The house was also pitch black. I flashed the light around in the kitchen to make sure that David Sloane wasn't lurking for me in the dark as Chocolate Delight had done. The floors on the first floor were of highly polished redwood. I took off my shoes so as not to arouse anyone who might be in the home. I had the 9mm pistol in my hand. It took me about 10 minutes to go through twenty rooms and three bedrooms that constituted the large country home.

I put my shoes back on and entered the basement through a door in the kitchen. I was certain that I would find Mrs. Chester down there dead. What I found is permanently etched in my mind and will haunt me for the rest of my days. Sitting upright on a work bench that was covered with a shower curtain, was the decapitated head of Irene Chester. Her mouth was gaped open with a three inch pipe. A pair of bloody vice grips lay next to the head. There was a molar locked between the jaws of the grips. The rest of Mrs. Chester's teeth, with the bloody roots intact, were scattered around the work bench. David Sloane was in the midst of destroying and obliterating of Mrs. Chester. A bloody, diminutive, headless skeleton with the heart and lungs still attached lie near a drain at the center of the unfinished basement. There were pieces of flesh still clinging to the skeleton. A bloody hatchet, axe, and machete were lying at the foot of the skeleton. David Sloane had hacked as much flesh off of Mrs. Chester's body as he could. The chunks of flesh were placed in seven small garbage bags, lined along the east wall of the basement. The basement was a bloody mess and smelled like a morgue as putrefaction set into Mrs. Chester's dead organs and flesh. It was the work of a true madman. I nearly threw up my daughter's and Mrs. Jackson's dinner when I opened one of the bags which had contained the bloody and fetid bowels and hunches of Mrs. Chester. I went upstairs and outside through the garage to get some fresh air and to get Cindy.

"Irene Chester's in there dead and decapitated," I said to Cindy. "Hacked to pieces." Cindy gasped and said, "Oh my goodness, Mack. What are we going to do?"

"We are going to go back in there and try to find that damn tape and get the hell out of here. That's what we're going to do." I said. "I think I know where he may be keeping the tapes. There's a room with several computers and printers on the first floor. That's where we'll start first."

"Let's go Honey," Cindy said. I don't want the nut coming home and catching us in his house."

"If he does," I said. We'll have to shoot him on sight. He's insane!"

We found the tapes right away. Sloane had made twenty copies and had them packaged and addressed to different media outlets. He already had the tape copied onto the website he had constructed and all he had to do, according to Cindy, was send his site out into the net. Cindy knew a great deal about computers. I was a novice. My knowledge only extended to what I needed to know in order to keep my files in order and to run the day-to-day operations of the office, but I was learning. Melissa was teaching me.

As I had previously surmised, David Sloane never had any intentions of giving the tape to Valerie. All along his plan was to embarrass and humiliate his brother and sister-in-law. I still wasn't sure that he was planning to kill Valerie, but if that tape had come out, he would have been the one who brought about her death; for even if she had not died physically, socially and emotionally he would have killed her. His hatred and envy of his brother apparently ran deep. He was willing to bring shame and embarrassment on his entire family in order to spite his brother. I wondered what slight - real or imagined - had propelled David Sloane on his reckless quest to destroy his brother and sister-in-law.

Cindy said that she had erased and deleted everything pertaining to Valerie from the computer, but she suggested that we take the hard drive as well because an expert would be able to retrieve certain data from it. Therefore, we took the hard drive and the hard disk, and all copies of the tape and fled the premises.

Sloane was a psychopath of the first degree and was, therefore unstable and unpredictable. I had no idea how he would react when I confronted him with the knowledge that I was aware of his abominable deeds, including the gruesome murder of Irene Chester. Cindy did not want to tangle with him at all. Since we had the tapes, she wanted us to call the police immediately and let them know that there was a dead body in David Sloane's basement.

"We have the tapes, Mack." Cindy said. "Our job is over, Honey. Let's just call the police and let them handle it from here. We can go to a pay phone. It will be an anonymous tip."

"The thing about calling in an anonymous tip on such a man as David Sloane is that it might be interpreted as a prank call, especially since it would be coming from a pay phone." I said. "In addition, if the police do go to his house now, he may somehow elude them. Judging from what he's done to Mrs. Chester, we can't risk letting him go. We have got to apprehend him tonight. If we sent them to the party, we may be jeopardizing the lives of innocent people including Alfred and Valerie Sloane. We know that he is volatile and emotional. We have to proceed with extreme caution. He has already mutilated a helpless old woman. What do you think he would do if he knew he had been found out and that he had nothing to lose?"

"What do you intend to do then, Mack?" Cindy asked. "We just can't walk up and put the cuffs on him. He's bound to resist and he may be able to convince others at the party to assist him. Then we'll really have hell on our hands. They're his family and friends, not ours."

"We're going to wait until the party's almost over and the guests have begun to leave. Then I'll try to lure him into a den or study under the pretense of discussing real estate with him. I'll be able to tell whether he is packing a pistol by the way that he moves around the room and the usual tell-tale bulge displayed by the amateur. It'll mean that we'll have a lot of explaining to do to the cops, but it can't be helped. We can't allow that maniac to leave the party and discover that he has been found out."

I turned into the Sloane estate. The gates were open in anticipation of the arrival of the guests. "I want to be with you Mack, to back you up." Cindy said. "You shouldn't take the chance of confronting him alone. He'll be desperate and subject to do anything to escape, as you've said."

I didn't want Cindy to accompany me for just that reason, but what she said made sense. In a gun fight, two guns are better than one. If it wasn't for my feelings for Cindy, I would have never thought about confronting Sloane alone when I had Cindy as back up. I hadn't hesitated before to place her in situations that we both knew could result in injury or death. The reason why I hadn't hesitated before was because I knew that Cindy would handle her business like a true professional if things got rough. Realizing that I was being overly protective now because she was to be my wife, I relented and allowed her to back me up, but it didn't sit well with me.

Sitting in the car we concocted a story that we would use on Sloane to lure him into a secluded area of the mansion, away from the remaining Sloane family and guests. At the right time, we would tell him that we had two million dollars to invest in real estate. We thought that would be a sufficient amount to arouse his interest.

CHAPTER 24

It was nearly 9 o'clock when we began our walk up the stone steps to the Sloane mansion. The fifty-four room Georgian edifice was indeed impressive. Six huge white columns supported the massive portico roof. The huge front doors of the mansion were carved red oak. They were ornamented with brass lion head knockers and brass door handles and locks. Expecting a doorman in full regalia, we were pleasantly surprised when Valerie Sloane, the perfect hostess, greeted us at the door. She was beautifully attired in a lavender silk and chiffon gown. She wore matching suede pumps. She wore her hair straight and pulled back from her lovely forehead and temples into a perfectly symmetrical braid that hung to her mid back. It was intertwined with silk lavender ribbons. She was the epitome of style, sophistication and grace and through her smile, she ignited the room. But, there was a subtle tension to her face and sadness in her eyes. What weight she must have been carrying on those delicate shoulders. She was holding her head high, but she knew that any moment her house could go tumbling down.

The shimmering crystal chandeliers and white marble floors interspaced with rich Persian carpets, upon which sat emerald, gold, and maroon colored sofas and chairs, grave the room a look of royal opulence. Looking around the room, there were about fifty well attired people in attendance.

"You're absolutely gorgeous in that gown, girl." Valerie said to Cindy. I could tell that Cindy had not expected to receive such a compliment from Valerie.

"Thank you." Cindy said. "But you know you got me beat. You must be the most beautiful woman that I have ever seen," Cindy said truthfully. Valerie blushed deeply and brought her hand to her mouth and said, "Thank you, Cindy. You're very kind to say so. I was beginning to fear that you two couldn't make it. Mr. Henry, by the way, you look real good in that tuxedo."

A lesser man - and a fool considering that my fiancée was right there - would have become discombobulated by Valerie's beauty and charm, but I managed to retain my composure and said, "Thank you, Valerie. That is quite a compliment coming from you, the most beautiful woman in the world."

Valerie simply said, "Thank you, Mr. Henry. I appreciate the compliment." She knew not to say too much with Cindy standing there.

"We have good news," I said unwilling to let Valerie go another second stressed by the thought that her naked body might appear on the internet in a pornographic video. Hope cut through the tension in her eyes and face and she asked, "What is it? Have you found the tapes?"

"Yes, girl." Cindy couldn't help interjecting. "We have the tapes and you don't have to worry about Pig no more. His foul ass is dead." Valerie laughed as if someone was tickling her and said, "Thank you. Thank you so much. You just don't know what this means to me. You have saved my life. Thank you so much!" She almost began to cry then looked around furtively, realizing that it wasn't the time or place for tears. "The tapes are out in the car - the original and the copies." I said. "We are going to destroy them as soon as we leave here."

Valerie's face was truly glowing and happy. I wouldn't have thought it possible, but the woman became even more lovely and beautiful with the news. I dreaded ruining her happy state by telling her that it was her own brother-in-law who was actually behind the plot to destroy her life. I decided to wait to the last possible moment. I even entertained the thought that I might still be able to convince David Sloane that Valerie had been an unwilling victim of the sex video. He was still going down for murder, but I thought that I still had a chance to convince him to leave Valerie out of it. I am optimistic by nature.

"Let me introduce you to my husband," Valerie said. "He has been especially anxious to meet you, Mr. Henry, ever since I told him that you were coming.

Dr. Slone looked more like a male model for Gentlemen's Quarterly Magazine than he looked like a brain surgeon. He was copper toned and stood over six feet tall. He was dapperly attired in a tailor-made black tuxedo with a black velvet vest. There wasn't a hair out of place on his carefully brushed jet black wavy hair. His mustache and slight beard were expertly lined and groomed. His patent leather shoes were shiny and new. He was rich, handsome, and intelligent. The kind of man every little girl dreams about; a prince in shining armor. In Dr. Sloane's case, shiny shoes.

"Good evening, Mr. Henry." Dr. Sloane said. "I've heard and read so many good things about you. I truly appreciate you and admire you for the help and service that you have rendered t the African American community here in Colorado and in Denver, in particular."

"Thank you, Dr. Sloane." I said shaking his extended hand. "It is, indeed a pleasure to meet you. My family and I have been proud of you and your family's achievements for quite some time. The fact that you give back to the African American community enhances your stature in our eyes."

"Thank you, Mr. Henry. I do the best I can. It is a duty instilled in my siblings and I by our father and grandfather."

Cindy and Valerie excused themselves and Dr. Sloane and I chatted for another 20 minutes or so. He was interested in several of the major cases that I had solved and which had been the subject of news reports and newspaper articles. I had been somewhat surprised by his knowledge of and interest in my work. He made me feel as though what I was doing was very important for the people of Colorado. At the end of our conversation, we exchanged numbers and Dr. Sloane had promised to send any business he could my way. We were also on first name basis. I hated to have to arrest his brother, but it could not be otherwise.

I made my way over to Cindy who was being admired by two men - one white, the other Asian. I think he was an Indian or Pakistani.

"If you'll excuse me, gentlemen," Cindy said. "My fiancé has arrived. Thank you for keeping me company while he was away."

"The pleasure was all ours," said the brown-haired, blue eyed white man. The Asian fellow looked upset and stalked off. He must have been up to no good, I thought. If I had not had more pressing business to attend to, I would have questioned him about his thoughts.

Cindy and I compared observations. We had both seen David Sloane periodically throughout the evening. He displayed all of the characteristics of the true psychopath. He didn't appear to be the least bit perturbed over the heinous murder he had recently committed, nor did he appear to be in any way bothered by the misery and shame that he thought he was about to unleash on his brother and sister-in-law.

We were all summoned into the massive dining room at 10 o'clock. It was a catered affair. We were served a meal of salmon, lobster, and crab cakes. There were all kinds of fruits, vegetables and salads and foods that I didn't even know the name of. The chocolate frosted banana cake was extraordinarily delicious. The butterscotch ice cream was something to savor.

David Slone and his apparent date had sat across from Cindy and me, two seats to the right of us. It was 11:15 when we decided to try to lure him into one of the many rooms of the mansion. Half the guests had departed and ten others or so were making preparation to leave. We couldn't allow David to leave the mansion and discover that someone was on to him.

"Mr. Sloane," I said across the table. That's when I received a glimpse of the other David Sloane - the maniacal, demon-possessed Sloane, for he looked at me with such evil and hatred that I momentarily considered following Cindy's advice to call the police and let them deal with this crazy man. Just as quickly, however, as David revealed his other self he concealed that self and a genuine looking smile replaced the demon possessed look and he said in a very pleasant voice, "How may I help you, Mr. Henry?"

Though we had not been formally introduced he knew my name. It was possible that he had heard of me as his brother had through the media, but it also dawned on me that we had seen each other in person before, only that time David was wearing a wig and a fake beard and was pretending to walk with a limp. Then I remembered the black Escalade that had obstructed my view of Valerie's Lexus as she drove east on south Stout Street away from my office. Sloane must have followed Valerie to my office and knew that I was on the case all along. Sloane was insane but he wasn't stupid. He was on to me before I was on to him. I watched Sloane from then on as if he were a poisonous snake for whose venom there was no antidote. Sloane was crafty. I would have to be extremely vigilant for surprises.

"Well, Mr. Sloane…" I started saying when David interrupted me and said, "Please call me David. Any friend of Valerie's and Alfred's is a friend of mine."

"All right then, David. Call me Mack. This is my fiancée, Cindy." I said playing along with his game. "We currently have over two million dollars invested in some mutual funds, stocks, and bonds.

We would very much like to invest in the sizzling real estate market. We're not experienced in the area, but we have heard that it is one of your areas of expertise. We do as much business with African Americans as we can because we discovered that the African American dollar doesn't circulate one time in its own community while in other ethnic communities their dollars circulate three to seven times before it leaves."

What I said concerning the African American dollar was true. I had studied the causes of black economic privation and the lack of black-owned businesses was a major contributing factor. We consumed too much and produced too little.

"That's right, Mack," David said warming to the subject. "My father taught my brother and me that we should always be keen for an opportunity to serve and enrich the black community."

"Is there a more private room that we might retire to in order to discuss this matter more confidentially?" I asked. "My fiancée is somewhat embarrassed to discuss our financial status in public."

"I understand, Mack. We can retire to my brother's study. It's just down the hall," David said rising and indicating the way with his right hand. While we were sitting at the table, Cindy had taken her .38 snub nose pistol from her garter and placed it in her purse. I had also taken the 9mm from my waist and placed it in my front pocket. I had intended to keep my finger on the trigger. If David did anything funny, I would blast him into the other world, the world of spirits.

CHAPTER 25

David led us into the study and directed us to two oversized leather chairs that stood in front of Dr. Sloane's massive mahogany desk. David took the chair behind the desk and poured himself a brandy from the crystal decanter that sat on the portable bar on his right. He didn't offer Cindy or me anything.

"Now," David said as he twiddled his thumbs over his interlocked fingers. "Just what type of properties were you two interested in? Condos? Apartments? Houses?"

Sloane spoke with a knowing smirk on his face. I decided to end our game of cat and mouse then and there and confront him with his nefarious deeds. I slowly eased the pistol out of my pocket as I began to answer David's question. Cindy took my cue and pretended to be searching for something in her purse.

"I'm interested in a chateau type property," I said standing and leveling my pistol at David's chest. Cindy stood on the other side of the desk and did the same. "One in which I might find the mutilated corpse of Irene Chester." Shock registered on his face and he was stunned to silence, so I continued. "The game is over David! We know that it is you who orchestrated the blackmail scheme against your own sister-in-law, Valerie Sloane. That it is you who have been tailing Valerie in Pig's Escalade!" I continued. "And it is you who killed and decapitated Mrs. Chester and then sadistically hacked the flesh from her skeleton." Yes, David, we have been to your home and have seen what you did to Mrs. Chester. And we have confiscated the scandalous video tapes which you intended to use to bring humiliation and shame to your brother and his wife and your entire family. Your real estate, banking and car dealing days are over. You'll be spending the rest of your life in prison or an insane asylum for what you did to Irene Chester!"

Upon hearing those words, the maniacal, demon possessed David reappeared; his erstwhile handsome face becoming hideously contorted by rage. His eyes seemed to bulge from his head as thick veins appeared across his forehead and temples. His lips twisted into a sinister sneer. If I wasn't a full grown man, I would have been afraid of David Sloane. Out of the corner of my eye, I saw Cindy's hand involuntarily convulse then steady itself. Then again, just as suddenly, David's face relaxed and he began to weep so childlike and pitifully that he nearly moved me to compassion. Then he said, "He was always my father's favorite. He went to every one of Alfred's football and basketball games. He left all of the houses, the mansion and most of his money to Alfred. I have always been the runner-up in my father's eyes. I was never good enough. He encouraged my brother to follow in his footsteps as a physician but he didn't seem to care what I did."

David sobbed bitterly for about thirty seconds and then, just as suddenly, he changed again. This time, when David spoke, the depths of his insanity became manifest. "I would have killed you the day that my whorish sister-in-law came to your office," David said nearly shouting as he rose to his feet. "Who in the hell do you think you are, meddling into my affairs? I am not to be trifled with Mr. Henry, and you'll soon discover that!"

David spoke to me as if I did not have a pistol leveled at his chest and, as if he thought that he would not be made to answer for the brutal muter of Irene Chester. Sloane was in denial. He could not face the fact that life as he had known it was over. Ignoring David's delusions of grandeur, I asked him the question that troubled me ever since I found out that Sloane was behind the plot to expose Valerie and humiliate his family. "I just have a few questions, David, if you don't mind answering them, because I am puzzled by your behavior. You are an enigma to me," I said knowing he would not be able to resist an opportunity to justify his deviant behavior.

"Ask what you will, Mr. Henry. But, I doubt that your feeble mind will be able to comprehend the profoundly intelligent actions of a man of my character," David Sloane said as he folded his arms and leaned against the bookshelf behind him.

Sloane was a megalomaniac who thought that his actions were beyond reproach. In fact, such people think that they are above the law and mores of society. I resisted the urge to challenge his boasted intelligence and proceeded to ask him the question that had perplexed me ever since I realized that David intended to circulate the scandalous videotape regardless of the consequences and repercussions to his family's name and reputation.

"Why would you want to humiliate your brother by showing his wife being raped and sodomized to the world?"

"That bitch wasn't being raped! Pig told me that she loved what he did to her - that she couldn't get enough of him," Sloane retorted.

"You see how ugly and repulsive Pig was, and you know how beautiful Valerie was. What in the hell would make you think that, out of all the people in the world whom she could have given herself to, that she would give herself to Pig? No, David. She was being raped. She was made to say those words you heard her say on the tape. Her mother had been pimping her out to Pig since she was ten years old just to get her daily fix of heroin. When her mother died from an overdose and Pig no longer had a hold over her, she escaped from him and began a new life with the help of some righteous people. Did you know that?" I asked David looking into his hate twisted face.

"No, I didn't know that and I don't give a damn. My brother has bragged about her virtues, how beautiful she was; so beautiful and pure; still a virgin at age 24 and all. But I know that hood rat bitch was too good to be true. That's why I had her investigated and found that she was a poverty stricken whore from the Roundville

Projects. That bitch should have come clean and revealed her shady past!" Sloane said with inhumane viciousness.

"If you had been sodomized," I countered, "From the time that you were ten years old until you were eighteen, would you publicize it? Would you want your fiancé or anyone else to know? Would you want anyone to know that your mother was strung out on drugs that she sold you for a fix? You have no right to think for her. She was a child when those things happened to her. As an adult, she has striven mightily to put her abusive and demeaning past behind her."

"Boo hoo!" David mocked.

"But you still haven't answered my question, David." I said ignoring his childish antics. "Or is it that you don't have an answer? Why would you humiliate your brother with such a vile tape?"

"I wanted to bring the pompous nigger down a notch or two!" Sloane hissed venomously. "He has always thought that he was better than me. Therefore, I wanted to show the world that the great, illustrious brain surgeon, Dr. Alfred P. Sloane, was married to one of the biggest whores in Denver."

Even though David was cultured and educated, he still considered his brother to be a nigger. He still thought of Dr. Sloane, whose brilliant mind had saved the lives of many, a nigger. I was shocked; shocked beyond belief.

"Then what is your justification for killing Mrs. Chester?" I asked. "Surely she posed no threat to you."

"That ignoramus, Pig, killed her when he told her the nature of our business and revealed my true identity to her. I told him not to tell anyone about me. Nevertheless, when I heard that he was dead, I went to her house to see if she required anything as far as assistance with funeral arrangements and such. She became hysterical and accused me of causing her son's death with my blackmail scheme. She threatened to go to the authorities and reveal everything. I could not allow that to happen, so I killed her." Sloane spoke as if he were talking about a fly or mouse.

"How did you lure her to your house?" You couldn't have killed her in her apartment." I said, getting the facts in case I had to give a statement to the police.

"She said that I had taken away her only means of support. She said that there was no one left to take care of her. I would have, but I could not be sure that she wouldn't eventually betray me. I told her that I would be a son to her from then on and have a maid and everything to do her shopping. She got her dumb ass in the car and the rest you already know."

Sloane then fell backward against the bookshelf and disappeared behind it as it gave way. He had slithered behind it as quick as a snake; neither Cindy nor I had time to react. It was difficult to shoot an unarmed man. Even one of David Sloane's detestable character. It turned out that the Sloane's had a secret chamber designed to shelter the family in the event of a home invasion. The room locked on the other side and we were unable to get into it. In about 30 seconds we heard a loud boom.

CHAPTER 26

After Dr. Sloane fanatically hacked a hole in the bookshelf wall with an ax and slid the bolt from the socket that fastened the door on the inside of the chamber, he found that David Sloane had blown the top of his head off with one of two shotguns kept in the secret chamber for the family's protection. Dr. Sloane and Valerie were beside themselves with grief.

"Good God!" I thought. What more could a man have wanted? He was rich and successful. David could have had his choice of any number of beautiful and suitable women. But, the Cain syndrome in David had been deep. He wanted to destroy his own brother, whom he envied and hated. Some people were never satisfied no matter what status they achieved in life. Instead of comparing himself with the billions of people who were less fortunate than himself, he tortured himself into insanity by comparing himself to his brother whose honor and prestige and wife he coveted. Obviously he thought his brother's attained status was beyond his reach; what a tragedy.

Cindy and I pretended to be oblivious to any motive David Sloane may have had to take his own life, but Valerie eventually figured things out. Two weeks after David killed himself; we received a check in the mail for $100,000 along with a letter which read:

My husband and I don't know how to thank you for everything you have done for us and by preventing a major scandal from destroying our family name and reputation. We also realize that David was deeply troubled and we have forgiven him. May he find peace.

I confessed everything to my husband and he still loves me and wants me to remain his wife; we cried together. I should have told him a long time ago but the little girl in me was scared and thought he would hate me and put me out of his house. Alfred is kind and loving and understands that what happened to me was not my fault.

We hope that this check will in some way compensate for you and your heroic efforts on our behalf.

Your friends for life,
Alfred and Valerie Sloane

Cindy and I got married three weeks later. We nearly spent the entire check we received from the Sloane's. Melissa looked like an angel in her pink and white flower girl dress. Mrs. Jackson approved of Cindy as a mate. She said, "It's about time you brought a woman into the house to help raise my grandbaby!"

I made love to Cindy for three days straight. We only got out of bed to shower, eat and change the bed sheets. I won't describe Cindy's naked body to you but let it suffice to say that it was very stimulating and pleasing to the eyes. Melissa flew to Rio de Janeiro two weeks later to join us on our honeymoon. She was truly happy!

The police have many theories as to why David Sloane killed himself and Mrs. Chester. The most widely published one stated that the younger Sloane had been involved in drug trafficking and that he killed Irene Chester when she threatened to disclose his involvement in the drug trade. She also blamed him for the death of her son. This came to light after Pig's Escalade and Mrs. Chester's body were found at David's home. They were wrong but if we explained what really happened, we would have had to disclose Valerie's secret life of abuse; something we would never do.

Solo's mom went into rehab and was doing ok. I helped them get a small apartment in Park Hill. Cindy helped Solo make out a budget and they were living well off of the money we gave them on a monthly basis. They had $15,000 left in their account after purchasing clothes and furniture for the apartment. I was also mentoring Solo, whose real name is Ricky Knight. He says that he wants to be a detective.

The two girls, Cindy and Bell, were placed in a foster home and Cindy and I visit them often. They each had $25,000 in a mutual fund that they would be able to access at age eighteen. I couldn't save the world, but I was doing my part to give some of our children a chance to grow and develop their minds uncorrupted by drugs and sexual abuse.

About the Author

Jeffery Alexander is known to most people as Abdullah (servant of God). Born in Birmingham, Alabama, he is the second son of a Baptist Minister. He spent most of his childhood and teenaged years in Denver, Colorado and Chicago, Illinois, respectively.

Unfortunately, he fell prey to the plight that befalls many of our young black men and began engaging in criminal activity at an early age. After receiving a harsh sentence for armed robbery, what was meant to break him had the opposite effect. It strengthened his resolve to redeem himself and to be the man he was destined to be from birth.

While incarcerated, he educated himself and earned Certificate in Small Business Administration, an Associates of Science Degree and a Bachelor's Degree. He served as the Imam (minister) for the Muslims in every prison in which he was confined. Having undergone transformation himself, his primary objective is to transform dark hearts and minds and to inspire people -- especially black people -- to love themselves and their own kind.

He wrote this street fiction novel, *Blackmail, Black Queen: 'til death do us part*, in hopes that the characters, exhibiting heart, feelings and soul, will allow people to identify with them and experience - vicariously - their trials and triumphs, victories and defeats.

He has written other pieces, a short story entitled "Alexandria" which was published in a national magazine and several articles in Prison publications and newsletters.

He plans to continue to let his voice be heard in a manner that will keep other young, black men from travelling the same path that he followed.

He is married to his childhood friend and confidant, Greta (Malika).

www.ingramcontent.com/pod-product-compliance
Lightning Source LLC
Chambersburg PA
CBHW071247130626
46556CB00003B/1200